Dragon's Bait

Books by Vivian Vande Velde

Vivian Vande Velde

Dragon's Bait

Magic Carpet Books
Harcourt, Inc.

Orlando Austin New York San Diego Toronto London

www.HarcourtBooks.com

First Magic Carpet Books edition 2003
First published 1992

Magic Carpet Books is a trademark of Harcourt, Inc., registered in the
United States of America and/or other jurisdictions.

The Library of Congress has cataloged the hardcover edition as follows:
Vande Velde, Vivian.
Dragon's bait/Vivian Vande Velde.
p. cm.
Summary: Wrongly condemned for witchcraft, fifteen-year-old Alys is
tempted to take revenge on her accusers when the dragon to which she has
been sacrificed turns out to be an ally.
[1. Dragons—Fiction. 2. Revenge—Fiction. 3. Fantasy.] I. Title.
PZ7.V2773Dr 1992
[Fic]—dc20   92-3761
ISBN 0-15-200726-1
ISBN 0-15-216663-7 pb

Text set in Fournier
Designed by Cathy Riggs

H G

Printed in the United States of America

To the members of my writers group,
without whom nothing would get done

Dragon's Bait

Chapter 1

THE DAY ALYS was accused of being a witch started out like any other.

She woke to the gray light of dawn and to the sound of her father coughing. Did he sound any better than he had the morning before? *Yes,* she told herself—*just a little bit, but definitely better.* And though she'd thought that every morning since late winter when he'd been so sick she'd been afraid he'd die, and though here it was with the wheat already harvested and the leaves beginning to turn, and he still too frail to run the tin shop by himself—that did nothing to lessen her conviction. He definitely sounded better.

Of course, it wasn't normal for a girl to help in her father's business. A man without sons was expected to take in apprentices, not teach his trade to a fifteen-year-old daughter. But her father had had no need for an apprentice before he got sick, and now there was nothing extra with which to afford one. Without the goat cheese that Vleeter and his wife had given them and the bread that the widow Margaret had periodically left at their doorstep, they might well have starved during those long, long days when he'd been too sick to work at all. So now he was teaching her how to draw out tin into wire, how to pour it to fashion buttons, how to cut and join. She was slow, just learning, and he was slow, having to rest frequently. Between the two of them they could craft just barely enough tin to keep themselves alive.

Until the day Alys was accused of being a witch.

It started in the late afternoon, when a man she didn't know came into the shop.

Saint-Toby's-by-the-Mountain was small enough that everybody knew everybody, so it wasn't often that she saw a stranger. She put down the shears with which she'd been cutting a sheet of tin and said, because her father had gone into the house to lie down, "Yes? May I help you?" It wasn't fair to judge someone by the way he looked, she knew, but there was something decidedly unpleasant about this man, about the way he didn't seem to fit together properly. The toothy smile didn't go with the cold eyes; the head, shaved in the manner of a man of the Church, didn't go with the long, elegant, beringed fingers; the clothes were much too fine for Saint Toby's—even for someone simply passing through Saint Toby's.

"You are Alys, the tinsmith's daughter?" the man asked, though his gaze was roving all over the shop and he must see who she was even if—she could tell—he disapproved.

Beyond him, she saw a flitter of movement by the door and recognized their neighbor, the wheelwright Gower. Now what was he doing? His shop had been closed all day, which was unusual, Gower being an ambitious man. He was so ambitious he had even made offers to buy their land so he could expand his own shop. His wife, Una, and their daughter, Etta, had refused to talk to Alys ever since her father had refused to sell. Leave it to Gower to show up at the first sign of trouble. "I'm Alys," she said.

"I am Inquisitor Atherton of Griswold,"

the stranger said, naming the town on the other side of the mountain. Alys's attention leaped back from Gower, but before she could say anything, he continued, "You have been accused of witchcraft, and it is my duty to prove that." The already insincere smile broadened. "Or disprove it, if the evidence so warrants."

"Witchcraft?" Alys had no idea what to say. "Who . . . I mean what . . . I mean . . ."

"You will come with me," the Inquisitor told her.

Alys knew she wasn't a witch and reasoned that she would therefore be proven innocent. Still, fear began to overcome confusion as Inquisitor Atherton took firm hold of her arm. Her voice shook. "But my father's aslee—"

The Inquisitor's fingers dug into her arm as he repeated, "You will come with me."

That was when she knew, deep in her heart—though she wouldn't admit it—that he would never find her innocent, no matter what. "Father!" she cried.

The Inquisitor pulled her out into the street. People were gathering to see what the stranger was up to. But out of all those faces, Inquisitor Atherton picked Gower. "Go fetch the father."

"Gower," Alys said, finally realizing.

And lest she have any lingering doubts, the Inquisitor was pulling her next door, to the storeroom behind the wheelwright's shop. "This will be our court," the Inquisitor said. "Gather those who would testify."

The room filled quickly. "What'd she *do*?" she heard several of the children ask. But the parents only told them "Hush," and looked at Alys with fear, while the whispered word "witch" played over the crowd so that she could never tell who had spoken it. She had known these people all her fifteen years. Surely they couldn't be afraid of *her*? But standing there among wheel rims and spokes of various sizes, with Inquisitor Atherton's grip bruising her arm, she couldn't be sure.

Her father came rushing in. Alys's heart sank, for she was alarmed by how pale he was. But Atherton wouldn't let her go and he wouldn't let her father approach.

"Stand there," the Inquisitor commanded her father. "Let it begin."

Let what begin? Alys wanted to ask, but she only had time to draw breath.

"I saw her"—Una's loud voice cut through

the murmuring of the crowd and everyone turned to face her—"in the street in front of Goodwife Margaret's cottage. I saw her look around to see if anybody was watching, but she didn't see me because I was bending over in my garden. She made a sign, and then she spat on the ground, and the next day Margaret's goat went dry and it's been dry ever since."

"I never—," Alys started.

"Be silent!" the Inquisitor warned.

"I will not," Alys protested. "What she's just said simply isn't true." She took a step toward Una, and Una threw her arms up in an exaggerated gesture as though to protect herself.

"Don't let her make the Sign against me!" Una cried, hiding her face.

"That's the most ridiculous—"

Before Alys could finish, Atherton grabbed her by the arm and dragged her away from Una. "We need a rope to bind her," he said. "And keep the father back."

"Don't hurt him!" Alys cried, seeing Gower shove her father, who'd been struggling to get to her. Atherton twisted her arms behind her back, and she felt rope being wrapped around her wrists.

Once she was tied, Atherton spun her around to face him. "Another attempt to harm the witnesses will be dealt with severely."

"But I didn't, and my father's sick, and—"

He put his finger close to her face. "Speak out of turn again, and *that* will be dealt with severely."

Alys jerked away from his finger but didn't dare answer. She looked at her father and tried to tell him with her expression not to worry, but she was too worried herself to be convincing.

It was Margaret who stepped forward, though she was almost half Atherton's height and probably twice his age. "Well, if she can't talk, I will," Margaret said. "What Una said is total nonsense."

"Has your goat gone dry?" the Inquisitor asked.

"Yes, but—"

"And it was a good milker before?"

"Yes, but—"

"Next!"

"I seen her," Gower said before Margaret could protest again. Everyone turned to look at him. "I seen her this past Midsummer's Eve. I just come back from fixing Barlow's cart wheel.

They had me to supper and I stayed late." He turned to Farmer Barlow. "You remember?"

Barlow was watching the Inquisitor and looking nervous about being involved. "I remember you coming."

"The moon had risen," Gower continued, "and I seen her plain as day in the meadow beyond Barlow's pasture. *What's she doing there?* I said to myself. She had her arms out like this and she was just turning round and round, like she was dancing real slow. I stood a moment, just wondering what she was doing. And then..."

"Then?" the Inquisitor said.

"She took her clothes off."

Horrified, Alys protested, "I never—"

The Inquisitor raised his hand as though to slap her. "Gag her," he commanded.

"No, wait," Alys gasped. "Please. I promise to be quiet."

Atherton changed his upraised hand to a gesture of warning. He turned back to Gower. "Then what?"

"She danced faster and faster, in a frenzy. A lewd, devilish dance. And then I could hear the sound of pipes playing high and sweet almost beyond hearing. Fairy music, I reckoned. Not something a man who believes in the good word of God should listen to. Nor see, neither."

Atherton turned to Farmer Barlow. "And you, have you heard or seen something a man who believes in the good word of God shouldn't?"

Barlow's gaze shifted nervously from Atherton to Gower to Alys, back to Atherton, as though searching for the safest answer. "I ain't seen nothing," he said, licking his lips. "But then, that meadow's to the back of the house."

"I've seen something," Etta said, "something half the people in Saint Toby's saw and heard."

"And what's that, my daughter?" the Inquisitor said, sweet and gentle.

"She went to the carpenter's shop, to have a stool made. After it was done, she and apprentice Radley had a big argument about the price. We all heard her. 'That's too much,' she said. 'I could make a better one than that,' she said, 'in fact from now on I will.' Several of us were gathered around the door to see. She pushed past me on the way out, but then I saw her turn back. And the moment she did, the *moment* she did,

Radley's chisel slipped and he gouged his hand something terrible so that he was hardly able to work for almost half the rest of the month."

"Is Radley, the carpenter's apprentice, here?" Atherton asked. "Step forward and tell us: Is this how it happened?"

Radley shuffled his feet and wouldn't look up, neither at Atherton nor at Alys. Tilden, the master carpenter, stood silent, next to him. "It's true," Radley mumbled.

"Who witnessed this argument and the aftermath?" Atherton demanded.

Hands raised, some reluctantly, some eagerly.

"What else?" Atherton asked.

And so it went.

Alys watched as one by one the friends who tried to defend her were bullied or frightened into backing down.

If only fat, jovial Father Joseph were still here, Alys thought. 'And did she dance naked even though it rained?' he would have asked. 'And isn't Goodwife Margaret's goat almost as old as Goodwife Margaret herself? And how often has apprentice Radley struck his thumb with a hammer and asked his master for the rest of the day off, and was young Alys there every time?' He might have dramatically clapped his hand to his brow and said, 'Last Sunday I forgot the words to my sermon. Maybe I've been bewitched, too.' Everyone would have seen how foolish the accusations were. Everyone would have noticed that Gower Prescottson and his wife, Una, and his daughter, Etta, were the only ones claiming to have actually seen her dance or spit or make the evil eye. Everyone would have laughed with Father Joseph.

But Father Joseph was dead, killed by the coughing sickness which had ravaged Saint Toby's this past winter, the same sickness that had left her father frail and bent over at the least exertion, so that now he could do nothing but put his thin hands over his face and rock back and forth where he stood.

Instead of Father Joseph, there was only Inquisitor Atherton. And Alys could see that he never laughed. Instead, he smiled. He smiled while Gower and his family told lies about her. He smiled while the confused villagers made vague comments about her. He smiled as they went from saying that she couldn't have done those awful things to saying that they didn't know anything about whether she'd done those awful things to saying that she may well have done those awful things.

It was only when the villagers were totally confused that he finally told her she could speak.

"I'm innocent," she started, "I—"

"Only the Blessed Virgin is innocent," Inquisitor Atherton bellowed. "Born into this world without blemish on her soul. How dare you compare yourself to the Mother of Our Lord?"

She heard her father groan. "But," she stammered, "but..."

"Do we burn her at the stake now?" Etta asked, unable to mask her enthusiasm. "Or do we throw her into the water first?" Water was sure proof. If the accused floated, that meant she was a witch and she was taken out and burned. If she sank and drowned, that meant she hadn't been guilty after all, and the village elder would apologize to any surviving members of the family.

Gower gave his daughter a dirty look. The last thing he needed at this point was a chance for Alys's name to be cleared.

But in any case Inquisitor Atherton was shaking his head. "We can solve two problems at once. A dragon has been terrorizing Griswold and the other villages on the north side of the mountain. It is a *small* dragon, as dragons go, contenting itself so far mostly with sheep and the occasional dog. Perhaps a *small* token of our respect will keep it from bothering the villagers themselves."

"Dragon?" Alys breathed. Her knees almost gave out under her. *I will not,* she commanded herself, *I will not give them the satisfaction.*

"Only a small one," Inquisitor Atherton repeated. With a smile.

In the end it was Alys's father whose knees buckled. Without uttering a sound, he clutched at his heart, then dropped to the floor and lay completely still. Nobody moved: perhaps because they were so surprised, but then again perhaps because he was father to a convicted witch.

Alys tore away from the two farm lads who had assigned themselves to guard her. Her hands were still bound behind her back, but escape was not what she had on her mind. "Father," she cried, throwing herself to the floor beside him. "Father!" But his chest no longer moved up and down with breath.

I will not beg for my life, she told herself, *and I will not let them see me cry.*

"Look at her," she heard some of them murmur. "Her heart is made of ice."

And others: "It's made of stone."

And again: "She's given it to Satan."

Someone jerked up on the rope that bound her wrists, dragging her up onto her feet. She forced her face to hide the pain. Instead she concentrated on the crucifix that hung on Inquisitor Atherton's chest, all gold and gems though she had never heard that Griswold was a rich town. She thought once again of Father Joseph, who had worn a cross his own father, a casket maker, had carved from wood.

"Get a cart to transport her," Inquisitor Atherton commanded. "We'll bury the old man when we get back."

And once more he smiled at her.

Chapter 2

It was dusk by the time Atherton called a halt to the parade that had followed out of Saint Toby's to the place where Alys was to meet her judgment.

It was also raining.

But despite the dark and the churned-up mud, Alys could see clear evidence of the dragon. First of all it looked like dragon country: fertile farms scattered about, a large nearby lake, a series of peaks and plateaus separated by deep valleys and crevasses and thick woodlands that would confound pursuit by those forced to go on foot rather than by wing. Alys had heard it all in ballads, and although she had never seen a dragon, had never met anyone who had personally seen a dragon, had never heard of a dragon in these parts in her lifetime, she recognized the signs: the trampled farms closest to the foot of the mountain, the scorched trees, the deep grooves—no doubt left by dragon claws—in a rocky outcrop by the lake. The cart horses kept tossing their heads and making nervous *huff* sounds and showing the whites around their eyes, as though something that only they could see or hear or smell spooked them.

Her mind shied away from the thoughts that crowded her. She tried to regain the image of her and her father. She pictured their heads together, with sunlight streaming through the shop window as he patiently explained tin craft to her as thoroughly as if she'd been born a boy and could really be his apprentice.

I will not give them the satisfaction, Alys repeated over and over, so afraid she could hardly think. But the repetition had kept her back straight during the journey as she'd sat in the cramped cart, which smelled of stale turnips. It had helped her to focus beyond the gawking faces and the jabbing fingers. And if her teeth and bones felt all rattled loose from the ride, surely the people who had walked, slogging those last miles through mud, were hardly to be envied.

They dug a hole, deep to go beneath the shifting mud, then set up a rough-hewn pole, tamping down the dirt to hold it fast. Gower pulled her from the cart, using more force than was needed considering she didn't resist. They never untied her arms, but ran another rope through the bindings and then around the pole.

"Iron's surer," Gower complained.

"Fey creatures have an aversion to iron," Inquisitor Atherton said. "We don't want to frighten the dragon away." Then he stood before her and bellowed, "Do not, therefore, let sin rule your mortal body and make you obey its lusts. No more shall you offer your body to sin as a weapon of evil. Rather, offer yourself to God as one who has come back from the dead to life, and offer your body to God as a weapon for justice. Then sin will no longer have power over you."

It was bad enough they were going to kill her; she wasn't going to let him twist Scripture to fit her. She spat at him, remembering what they had said about Margaret's goat. The action lost some of its effectiveness since he was already soaked with the rain and she couldn't even tell if she had hit him.

But Atherton could afford to be magnanimous. "Repent," he told her, "and save your immortal soul."

She stared beyond his right shoulder, to a place in her mind where dust motes played in the sunlight and her father's big but gentle hands guided hers over a piece of tin that would eventually become a cup.

Atherton was willing to be magnanimous, but he wasn't willing to get wet for nothing. He instructed them to stick some of the flaming torches into the ground so that the dragon wouldn't have any trouble finding her. Then he sketched the sign of the cross in her general direction and turned his back on her.

The villagers followed him, returning down the slope lest the dragon come and make a meal of them all. She could hear the creak of the cart and a snatch or two of excited chatter, and then the rain swallowed up the sounds as thoroughly as the shadows had swallowed the people themselves. The torches sputtered and smoked in the dampness.

I should have left them with a nice curse, Alys thought. *Something to keep them up nights, shivering in their beds.* But Alys didn't know any curses, and anyway it was too late now.

She found a position where she could lean against the pole without any of the rough places sticking into her back.

At least she was alone, and for a while that was a comfort. But she could no longer form the picture of her father's workshop. Pieces of it kept slipping away, like shards of tin falling to the floor. And when she'd concentrate on those elusive parts, force them into being, other things would dissolve until eventually she couldn't even picture her father's face.

Then, with no one there as witness, she finally cried.

EVENTUALLY THE RAIN stopped. Clouds like tattered rags raced across the face of the almost-full moon. Alys was certain the rope around the pole was loose enough that she could slide down to rest her legs, but she wasn't sure she could get back up. The pole had been shaped so quickly, so roughly, that it was likely to snag the bindings, and that would be a terrible way to die:

caught in a half-crouch, her bottom all muddy from sitting on the wet ground.

How would the dragon kill her? Perhaps she would be less afraid if she figured out just what to expect.

A blast of flame? *Not likely,* she decided. In the stories, dragons frequently asked for young maidens. If they simply incinerated their victims, why worry about age or gender or lack of...Alys's stomach tightened. Despite what Inquisitor Atherton had shouted at her about sin and lust and Satan ruling her body, she *was* a maiden. In the village of Saint Toby's, there were girls who had been born the same year as she who were already married; two of them— Nola, whose father had gone to sea and never returned, and Aldercy, who was wed to Barlow's second-youngest son—already had babies. But Alys had never had much use for the village boys, who had all seemed coarse and pushy and who never dreamed of anything beyond Saint-Toby's-by-the-Mountain and one day running their own fathers' shops. Alys had always thought...she'd thought...

What difference did it make what she had thought? Here she was tied to a pole as dragon's bait, and if the dragon ever got around to coming, it would kill her in some fashion that probably would not be with a blast of flame.

Which undoubtedly would have been the quickest.

In all likelihood it would eat her. The call for maidens could conceivably have something to do with the quality of taste. All she had to worry about was whether it would start to eat her right away, while she was still breathing and screaming and knowing what was going on, or kill her first, perhaps with a swift flick of those claws, which had cut through the stone by the lake, or maybe by biting off...

This wasn't helping. This was making things worse.

It would probably be fast, she tried to convince herself. *I won't cry again.* It wasn't enough that Gower and his horrid family and Atherton and all the rest couldn't see her, would never know: She wasn't going to cry again.

It *would* be fast. She'd seen the claw marks on the stone, the trees knocked out of the way of the creature's passing. It had a wingspan hundreds of feet across, and it was incredibly strong. It would be fast.

In the distance a wolf howled.

Alys shivered, a combination of the cold breeze through her rain-soaked clothes and the thought that a wolf wouldn't be fast.

The moon was no longer directly overhead. It wasn't exactly sinking below the horizon, but what if the dragon didn't come? What if she remained here for days, starving, fevered from the chill she was surely already catching? And what of wolves?

She twisted her arms and realized the rope that held her wrists was looser than she had anticipated. She tried to think back, to remember all the way to this afternoon and to who had tied her.

Perryn the wood-gatherer. Ah yes. Not that he was of a kinder disposition than the others, but he never could get anything right.

Alys folded her thumbs and little fingers in, trying to make her hands as narrow as possible. The twine rubbed painfully against her flesh as she tugged.

She yanked and nothing happened.

She pulled with steady pressure and felt the rope ease down over her right hand. Again she tugged.

This time her right hand came loose. She shook the tangle of knots off her left wrist, and that rope, still entwined with the rope that went around the pole, dropped in a heap to the mud at the foot of the pole.

Her arms felt as though they were going to fall off. The burning pinpricks of pain were so bad she almost wished they would. She flexed her fingers, her wrists, her shoulders—to get the blood moving again.

Now what?

She couldn't go back to Saint Toby's. They'd just bring her straight back here, and this time make sure she was tied securely. And even, she thought, *even* if they did take her escape as proof that she was innocent and forgave her, how could *she* ever forgive *them*, live with *them*, see *them* every day for the rest of her life knowing what they had thought, what they had caused to happen to her father, what they had wanted to do to her, what they still might do?

And she couldn't just go to a different village and try to make a new life. It wasn't like she was a boy with a trade, or even one who could be apprenticed. A very young girl child might be taken in on mercy, but she was too old by at least half.

Wrapping her sore arms around herself for warmth, Alys stooped down to ease her legs. She was no longer tied to the stake, but she had not really escaped for she had nowhere else to go.

That was when the dragon came.

Chapter 3

HER FIRST INCLINATION was to hope the dragon hadn't seen the torches and that she'd have time to run under cover of the nearby trees. It was hard to judge how high the creature was flying—above the treetops, below the almost-full moon—without knowing how big it was. And it *was* big, whatever the distance worked out to be. Its enormous wings carried it halfway across the sky with one powerful beat. The thing was close enough that she could see it had a mane, which she had never heard mentioned in any of the legends, but far enough away that she couldn't make out the individual scales.

Then she realized the dragon *hadn't* seen her, and that if she stayed still for a few moments longer, she was free. But she was soaked to the skin and cold, and she hadn't eaten since early morning—and here it was, almost dawn of the following day—and she was an orphan with nowhere, absolutely nowhere, to go. And she remembered the wolves.

Her choices, as she saw them, were to die quick or to die slow.

She chose quick.

Standing, she flung a rock with all her might. "You stupid dragon!" she screamed. "Come and get me!"

Her muscles, cramped and strained from being tied so long, rebelled. The rock arced and plummeted to the ground far short of the dragon. But her movement, or her shout, attracted its attention.

Probably the wrong choice, she thought, as the creature wheeled gracefully and glided back toward her. She closed her eyes and braced herself.

She felt the wind of its wings as it passed overhead, circling, perhaps suspecting a trap. Then it settled to the ground before her. She braced herself . . . braced herself . . . braced . . .

She opened her eyes just the tiniest bit, sure

that what she'd see would be her last sight: a tongue of flame about to engulf her, or great slathery jaws opened wide to tear her, or sharp claws about to rake the life out of her.

What she saw was the dragon's kneecap.

Momentarily she reclosed her eyes. She had expected the creature to tower over her; she just hadn't realized that it would tower over her even before its legs ended.

She swallowed and opened her eyes again. She tipped her head back, back, back.

The dragon watched her from that impossible height.

"Well, kill me," she whispered.

Still the dragon just stood there, pale in the light of the moon and torches, its wispy mane fluttering in the soft breeze, its eyes too far up for Alys to see more than a dark hint. It didn't smell of sulfur, which was something the balladeers almost always said, or of blood or carrion, which was something else she'd expected. More like damp meadow grass on a spring day.

Alys thought back to this past winter when so many people had gotten sick, which made her think of her father, who had survived, which made her think of him collapsing in Gower's storeroom, his hand to his chest. She kicked the dragon, hard.

The impact made her toes sting.

The dragon tipped its head slightly to one side as though considering. Something.

So, this wasn't going to be quick after all: The dragon was going to play with her. She should have chosen the wolves while she'd had the chance. But, from some unexpected place within, a giggle bubbled up. "Now, dear," she said, "don't play with your food." She covered her face with her hands and sank to the ground. She had so wanted to be brave, even if she was the only one who'd know it, and here she was laughing and sobbing at the same time, facing her death with her rear end in the mud after all.

With her eyes scrunched closed behind her hands, she was aware of the dragon moving. *This is it,* she thought. But still she jumped as something brushed her hand. *I'm sorry,* she thought desperately to God, not for being a witch, which they both knew she wasn't, but for anything else—she was too scared to think of specifics—the impatiences, the missed opportunities to go out of her way to be kind, the times she'd daydreamed during Mass, the...the... what? Her mind shut down, refusing to come up with anything. And what was this stupid dragon doing?

Just as she was trying to get up the courage to open her eyes, she realized that hands were pulling at her hands, uncovering her face.

Hands—not claws.

Alys gasped, opening her eyes and dropping her hands all at the same moment.

A young man, looking maybe two years older than she, crouched before her, his hands still on hers even now as they rested in her lap.

There was no sign of the dragon.

For the briefest moment she wondered if he were some sort of dragon-slaying prince who'd killed— No, there'd been no time for that— who'd frightened away...But there'd been no sound....

She looked again, and didn't know how she could have ever mistaken him, however briefly, for human.

The thing that was most obviously wrong were the eyes. And she thought that before she even noticed the color, which was that of the amethyst gem in the crucifix Inquisitor Atherton wore. *"It's a small dragon,"* Alys recalled Atherton saying. No wonder. If this human manifestation was any indication, the dragon wasn't fully adult yet. It gave her a perverse pleasure to think of the villagers of Saint Toby's having to contend with him when he reached his full size. Even if she wouldn't be alive to see it.

By the light of the torches she saw that his hair was the color the mane had been, palest gold, and it hung almost to his waist. Alys jerked her gaze back up to the face, for she had suddenly—finally—noticed that he wore no clothes.

For the first time, the purple eyes flickered with emotion: amusement. He had seen her discomfort, and recognized the cause.

"I didn't know," she said, to say anything, and looked away and simultaneously tried to pull her hands from his, "that dragons could take on human shape." She was surprised that her voice worked. His hands felt like human hands—the texture, the warmth, everything was just as it should be, but . . .

He refused to release her hands until she looked at him again. He smiled, but this time the amusement didn't reach his eyes. "It's not often," he said in a voice that was soft and husky, but well within the norms for a human of his—apparent—age and build, "that I find a damsel flinging rocks at me." He paused as though considering and slowly added, "It happened once with a knight, but I'd already eaten his horse and most of his weapons. The squire, too, as I recall." He tipped his head slightly as though waiting for a response, the same gesture he had made while in dragon shape.

"I see," Alys said.

He raised his eyebrows doubtfully.

Alys stared at her hands in her lap. Dragon or human, he certainly appeared human, and it was disconcerting to have him crouched before her with nothing on.

The dragon-youth sighed and sat down on the cold ground, his right leg folded under him, the left up so that he could rest his elbow on his knee, which afforded some modesty, if she didn't think about it. "Humans," he sighed in a tone that reminded Alys that—whatever was the dragon equivalent to seventeen years old—dragons lived for hundreds of years. "Sometimes I forget."

Alys glanced up and then away. Up long enough that she saw him nod toward the pole to which she'd been tied.

"That yours?"

She nodded, never looking up.

"You had time to get away."

She met his eyes then. Defiantly. "You didn't see me."

That stirred something deep beneath those cut-glass eyes, but it was already gone before he spoke. "Of course I saw you. I wasn't interested until you began to act out of the ordinary."

His superior attitude annoyed her despite her still very real fear. "People staked out on hillsides is ordinary?"

He flashed his cold grin. "It is for me."

She sucked in a breath, reminded of her earlier concern. "Why is it . . . ?" She hesitated, not sure she wanted to know.

"What?"

Maybe she was worrying needlessly. "Can all dragons change to human shape?"

He paused, as though considering how much to tell her. "No," he said, just at the point she realized she couldn't believe him, whatever he answered. "Only gold-colored dragons have magic." He repeated her own words to her: "'Why is it...?'"

She looked down again.

He forced her chin up.

In a very small voice, never meeting his eyes, terrified of the answer that she had so glibly dismissed earlier, she asked, "Why is it dragons ask for maidens?"

The dragon-youth released her, his hand shaking. Startled, she looked up and saw that he was silently laughing. "Dragons don't ask for maidens," he said. "Dragons are offered maidens."

Alys shook her head to show she didn't understand.

"Is a king likely to be a maiden? Or a village headman? It's the men who make the laws that decree that maidens be offered."

Alys thought of all the lovely old songs, the grieving kings, the valiant knights. "That's a lie," she whispered.

"Perhaps." She saw a glint in his eyes. "I *do* lie."

"Yes," she snapped at him, suddenly more angry than afraid, "just like the old riddle: Everything I say is a lie. But if that's true, then it's not a lie, so that makes it not true, which means it's a lie, which—"

The dragon swept to his feet, and Alys kept her gaze firmly on his face. "I didn't say *everything* I said was a lie. And I hate riddles. The last time a knight challenged me to a riddling contest, I lost. And then I ate him anyway. Why"— he leaned down with his hands on his knees to put his face on a level with hers—"didn't you run away when you had the chance, before I saw you?"

"You—" Alys had started to say, "You said you saw me all along," but she stopped just short of it.

Maybe he read her thought in her eyes.

She looked at her hands in her lap.

"Why didn't you run away?"

"To where?" she shouted. "I have nowhere to go. They killed my father. They convicted me of being a witch. I'm cold and wet and hungry." She gave a ragged sigh and lowered her voice. "And I have nowhere to go."

The dragon sat down again. "*Are* you a witch?"

"No."

"What are you going to do about it?"

"There's nothing I can do. Except enjoy the thought of you flying over Saint Toby's village and breathing fire and roasting them all, every single one of them, down to the last baby."

The dragon raised his brows.

"Well," she said, "maybe not the babies."

The dragon grinned and stood again.

Alys refused to look up.

The dragon gave an awful cry, like a huge bird of prey.

Alys jerked her head up and saw that he'd resumed his dragon form. Now she'd made him angry, failed whatever test it was he'd set, or simply no longer amused him. The great wings flapped with a sound like sails snapping in the wind, and she threw her hands up to protect her face.

The claws grasped her forearms and she gritted her teeth. But the talons didn't sink into her flesh, they raised her from the ground. Her arms felt as if they would be pulled from their sockets, reawakening the pain that had just begun to subside. Alys opened her eyes and saw that she was already dangling high, high up above the trees. She screamed in terror at the thought that he would drop her and she would plummet long moments before hitting the ground, or that he wouldn't drop her at all but was carrying her to his lair. She screamed again and again, too frightened to close her eyes against the stinging wind and the lurching countryside.

And then he did let her go.

The rushing air tore the scream from her throat, but she didn't fall for long. And the ground she hit was soft, bouncy. A haystack, she realized from the smell of it, and the prickliness, before the fog of terror cleared from her eyes.

She lay there flat on her stomach waiting, waiting, her heart beating so loudly she could hear nothing else.

A half-lifetime later she finally raised her head, saw that she was alone. "Where are you?" she screamed into the night. "What are you doing to me?"

The night didn't answer.

She lowered her face into the crook of her arm and rocked back and forth. Despite everything that had happened—because of everything that had happened—she drifted off to sleep.

Something dropped beside her.

She gasped, sitting up.

It was a rough-spun peasant dress and a sturdy pair of shoes that she had felt land next to her. The dragon, once again human-shaped, was crouched beside her, this time wearing clothes—a peasant's shirt and breeches. He nodded his head to where she had been lying. "I thought you were crying."

"No," she said. "I don't cry, ever."

His face showed nothing.

"Where'd you get these?"

He gestured off into the pink-edged dark. "Farmhouse."

"You didn't... kill the people? Did you?"

He paused, with that expression of his that said he was weighing his answer. "They'd run off. Abandoned the place."

She sighed in relief. "Really?"

He shrugged, with a condescending smile. "Perhaps. You better get out of your wet clothes."

"Turn around," she commanded.

He did, but she could see his shoulders shaking once more with silent laughter.

Chapter 4

ALYS FINISHED LACING the bodice of her
borrowed dress and looked up to find the young
man who was a dragon unabashedly regarding
her. No telling, from that bland expression, if
he'd turned a moment before she had, or if
he'd been watching all along. Warmth flooded
her cheeks, from anger and embarrassment. The
suspicion that he could see her blush, even in the
dim predawn light, made her angrier yet and
even more embarrassed. He sat too close to her,
but perched on the top of the haystack, she had
nowhere to go. She lowered her gaze to avoid
his face. Except for the color of the eyes, everything was just too right.

And nothing was right at all.

She concentrated on her anger, to give her

voice the bite it needed. "That's very rude, you know."

For a long moment he said nothing, as though in the interim he'd forgotten how to speak. Finally he said, "What is?"

"Watching me get dressed. People don't do that."

"Don't they?" he asked with just enough balance between polite inquiry and irony to show that he knew the truth of it.

"*Nice* people don't." He looked momentarily startled, as though taken aback that she could have ever confused him with someone who could be nice. His expression shifted to amusement. Before he could start laughing outright, Alys said, "And I don't like the way you sit so close to me, either." She regretted the words immediately for they gave him yet another advantage over her.

So she wasn't completely surprised when he seized her arm. But she wasn't expecting him to tug. Together they skittered and wobbled down the side of the haystack, sending flurries of hay flying till she landed in a heap, half on top of him, though she'd been sliding down haystacks for as far back into her childhood as she could remember.

Once she managed to figure out which end was up, Alys jerked her arm to break the dragon-youth's grip. He held on just long enough so that, when he did let go, she tipped over. She fell flat on her back, and more hay showered on her. Furious, she leaped to her feet and ineffectually brushed at the hay that was in her hair and clothes. Unsure how much of her discomfort was actually premeditated on his part, she snapped, "Thank you."

Still sitting at the foot of the haystack, he looked up at her but said nothing.

Surely it couldn't be that easy. "For everything," she added.

Still nothing.

So Alys turned and took a step away.

And a second.

And a third.

She braced herself for him to grab her from behind, knowing that he could move with uncanny speed and silence. She took another step, her shoulders involuntarily hunched in anticipation, cringing from the thought that he could transform himself as silently as he could move, and that it might not be with hands that he'd choose to catch hold of her.

She managed one more step.

When she turned, he was sitting as before, watching her. Her voice quivered. "Why are you doing this?"

He put on an expression that was a bit too much of wide-eyed innocence.

"What do you want from me?" she demanded.

Still he gave her nothing, as though waiting for her to choose the direction the conversation must take.

She returned to the haystack and sank down beside him. "I don't trust you."

Finally he reacted: He laughed, soft and throaty. "All for the best."

Trying to undermine her confidence, was he? In an attempt to appear equally mysterious and dangerous, she said, "And you shouldn't trust me."

He arched his eyebrows.

Alys worked to keep her chin level. "Just so we both know."

He inclined his head solemnly, though she suspected he didn't take her seriously. "Just so we both know," he repeated, his voice, as ever, telling her nothing.

"What do you want?"

He paused, perhaps considering what he could say that she would believe, perhaps working on regaining his sincere look. "To help you."

"To help me...?" If he had hoped to find something she would believe, he had failed. "That's very kind of you," she said bitterly, for she no longer believed in kindness. "And you're willing to do this... why? Because you're fond of helping others?"

"I'm fond of revenge," the dragon answered.

Alys sat back on her heels, considering. She had a fleeting image of her father clutching his chest, sinking, ever sinking, to the floor of Gower's storeroom. *Revenge.* Never once had the word actually formed in her mind, but now that the dragon had said it, she recognized the thought that had been with her all day. She remembered what she'd said, about roasting the village, babies and all. "You'd burn their fields, demolish their houses, devour the survivors?"

"Yours for the asking," the dragon said. He gave her his chilliest smile and advised, "Don't ask."

So there *was* a catch. "Why?"

"Revenge," the dragon said, "is sweetest when it's slow enough that the one doing it can see the results, and the one to whom it's done knows from where it comes."

She thought of Gower, and his wife, Una, and their daughter, Etta. And she thought of Inquisitor Atherton, and she nodded.

"Do you want my help?" the dragon asked.

She knew exactly what he was doing, forcing her to put it into words, to admit to it, to take responsibility for it. "Yes," she said, savoring the sound of the word.

There was a flicker of something across his face, something too fast, or too far removed from any human emotion, for her to recognize. Again she was left with the feeling of having just passed—or failed—some test. His voice gave no indication which. "Who do you most want to see suffer?"

"Gower," she said, almost before he'd finished the question. And again, more calmly, "Gower."

"Then, of course," said the dragon, "we'll have to do him last."

So she told him all of it. The lies spoken. The lies implied. Her father's death.

The dragon-youth listened to everything, never asking questions, never bringing her back to the main point when her story wandered to Father Joseph sprinkling holy water on the fields every spring or to her mother who'd died two days after Alys was born.

I'll tell him everything, Alys thought, *and when I'm done, he'll tell me what to do.*

But when she was done, the dragon only said, "We will go indoors now, since your human body is more fragile than mine." He was on his feet before she saw him start to move, as though he'd only been waiting for the sound of her voice to stop. As though he hadn't been listening to the words.

And was the reference to her fragile body a subtle threat, she wondered, masquerading as concern? Or concern, perhaps, masquerading as threat? She wasn't comfortable with either idea. Nor with the thought of being confined with him, trapped by walls.

Not that she was in any less danger out here.

Now would be a good time to run, to break away from him and hide. Without checking to see if she followed, he was already headed for the farmhouse to which this haystack no doubt belonged. But ... *was* he that confident that she would come, or was it just that he didn't care one way or the other? He had made no move to stop her before, after pulling her down the haystack. *Didn't* it make any difference? Was it all the same to him?

And her situation was certainly no better now than it had been on the hillside when she had first gotten loose from her bonds, before she had ever seen him. She had nowhere to run then, and she had nowhere to run now. Except that now she had told him her life story, and he had indicated—hadn't he?—that he would help.

He'd entered the cottage with never a backward look for her. He must have lit a fire earlier while getting the clothes, for cheery firelight spilled out of the doorway. She could make out that this side of the cottage—the front—was singed, and the door hung loose on one twisted hinge. Beyond, what had to have been the barn was a burned-out shell. If there had been anybody still alive in either building, surely they'd have been up by now, and out here to inquire about the presence of strangers in their haystack.

Of course, the fact that there was nobody alive didn't mean there was nobody in the cottage.

At the last moment Alys balked yet again, unwilling to confront proof that the dragon had lied to her in this. But if she had a chance—*if* she had a chance—it wasn't out here. Slowly she entered.

There were no bodies after all. Or at least none lying out in the open. In the light from the fire in the hearth, Alys could see that the contents of the cottage were strewn about, but it was impossible to tell whether that was from the owners trying to decide what to take in a hurry as they fled, or from looters, or from the dragon searching for clothes and not knowing enough of humans to guess where they'd be kept. Presumably a dragon would have no trouble lighting a fire.

Somehow he was behind her, close enough that when he spoke his breath stirred the hair that had come loose against her neck. "If you want," he offered, "I could fetch you something to eat."

She jumped and whirled to face him. "No," she answered so quickly that he smiled.

Annoyed, she turned her back on him and began searching for food. "See," she meant the set of her shoulders to tell him, "I'm not afraid of you." And when was he going to do something or say something about all that she had told him? She found a sack with three wrinkled apples left over from last autumn; and, though it was almost time for this year's crop, they looked like the most delicious things she'd ever seen.

"Do you—" She started to turn around, saw that he was just removing his shirt, and hastily kept on turning. She bit her lip, her heart pounding. "What are you doing?" she asked in a panic.

He didn't answer and didn't answer, and still she wouldn't look. Then she heard a sound that could only be a huge mass of talons and scales and tail settling down on the packed-dirt floor. She turned and found the dragon curled up like a cat, his tail around him and his chin resting on his paws, never mind that he took up almost the entire room.

"What if the owners come back?" she asked.

The dragon, who'd already closed his eyes, reopened them and looked at her, unblinking.

"What if the people from Saint Toby's return to make sure I'm dead?"

From outside she could hear the first twitterings of birds rousing themselves for day, though it was still dark out. The dragon closed his eyes again, ignoring her.

"I've told you everything about me," she cried, "all my secret dreams, everything I ever hoped for, all my fears and inner thoughts. I hate it when you act as though I'm not here."

He looked up at her with a flash of annoyance but still said nothing.

Alys opened her mouth, but then closed it as things became clearer. "You can't talk when you're not in human form, can you?" She sighed. "You should have said so before."

The dragon jumped to his feet, transforming so quickly that he had lunged and grabbed her arm before she realized that it was his hand and not a claw that held her. "Of course I can talk when I'm not in human form." His fingers dug into her arm. "I can talk the language of whatever beast I'm in the shape of: When I'm a horse, I talk horse. When I'm a hawk, I talk hawk. *When I'm a human, I talk human.*"

Wincing from the pain and the intensity, Alys objected, "Humans aren't beasts."

"*THEY ARE TO DRAGONS,*" he shouted. "And only a human would be arrogant enough to argue about it."

"Arrogant?" Alys was too angry to be concerned about him standing there naked, holding her close. "*Arrogant? You're* calling *me* 'arrogant'?"

The dragon put his face close to hers. His voice suddenly soft and dangerous, he warned, "Be careful you don't become more trouble than you're worth."

As far as she could tell, she was already more trouble than she was worth. She tugged to snatch her arm away and realized he'd only let go of her before because he'd been good and ready to let go; if it was a contest of strength, he wouldn't even be aware of the force she exerted against him. Her anger cooled to an icy lump in her chest. "I'm sorry," she said quietly.

There was nothing in his face to indicate what he thought of that, whether he was disgusted by her fear or if, like Inquisitor Atherton, he took pleasure in it.

"I'm sorry," she repeated, softer yet.

He took a step back from her, giving himself room to return into dragon shape, and she decided that meant he wasn't going to kill her after all.

"Wait." As soon as she said it, she realized that he could kill her just as well in either shape. Still, maybe she should act as though she assumed the best, just in case he hadn't made up his mind. She said, "If we're going to be working together, I can't very well call you, 'Hey, you, dragon.'"

He narrowed his purple eyes at her and must have weighed considerations about which she wasn't even aware. "You may call me Selendrile," he said with just the slightest hint of sibilance. A moment later he'd resumed dragon shape and once again settled on the floor.

"Selendrile," she repeated, tasting the sound of it. "I'm Alys."

The dragon opened his eyes just long enough to look bored, then went to sleep.

Chapter 5

BY THE TIME Alys woke up, it was dark again. There was still, or again, a fire in the hearth. The dragon—Selendrile—was awake and in human form and crouched beside her, close enough to touch. She flinched, thinking he'd been about to shake her awake and that if she didn't look alert fast enough he might yet. But then she realized he was too still; she hadn't caught him between motions after all. He was simply there watching her, with that appraising expression that made him look as though he'd been either trying to read her mind or speculating how she'd taste.

She scrambled to her feet. He stayed where he was, only tipping his head back slightly to continue watching her. "Don't do that," she demanded, recalling—even as she said it—having heard the younger children at Saint Toby's say much the same thing, in much the same tone. "Stop looking at me."

He looked neither amused nor annoyed. Nor about to comply.

She swept past him so she wouldn't have to admit to either of them that her words had no effect on what he did or did not do. Her stomach felt as though it were twisted in a knot, she was so hungry; and despite the fact that she had searched earlier and found only the three apples, scouring the cottage for food would take her mind off both Selendrile and the thought of how long it had been since her last meal.

She paused in midstride, seeing a large wooden bowl on the table, filled almost to the top with a thick stew. She suddenly realized that the warm smell of it—potatoes and chicken and barley—filled the small cottage, and her stomach clenched even tighter as her mouth began to water. "What's this?" she asked softly.

"It's called stew," the dragon said. "Assorted grains and vegetables and some meat, heated to the point where no one can tell which is which."

Alys turned to see if he was being sarcastic or if he really thought he was telling her something she didn't know. She couldn't be sure. "I meant, where'd it come from?"

Selendrile gave a slight tip to his head. "I got it from a farmhouse on the outskirts of town."

"*Got* it?" she asked.

"Stole it," he corrected readily enough. "I didn't know how long your human form could go without nourishment. You seemed to be too weak to rouse yourself and I thought you might be dying."

Again the not-so-subtle hint that she could never keep up with him. His speculation on her mortality was spoken in the same tone he'd used to describe the contents of the stew.

"I was just tired," Alys said, annoyed, and somewhat chilled despite the fire. "I hadn't slept at all last night. Don't dragons sleep?" She knew they did; she'd seen him at it. Except that apparently he'd kept at it for a much shorter time than she had. He'd waited for her long enough to consider the possibility that she wouldn't get up, to fetch nourishment, bring it back here, and be crouched for who-knew-how-long staring at her until she'd opened her eyes.

Selendrile didn't answer, as though he couldn't be bothered with affirming something he knew she already knew.

Alys wondered whether—if she *had* died—he'd have eaten her, and if that was why he'd been waiting so patiently by her side. "Thank you," she said, sitting down at the table. "For the food."

Again he didn't answer.

"Are you going to eat some with me?"

"I've already fed."

And looking down into those cold amethyst eyes she had no idea if he'd eaten some of the stew or the person who'd prepared it. She forced down a mouthful that seemed intent on lodging itself in her throat. *He's never going to let you live,* a small part of her warned. *He'll help you get revenge on Atherton and Gower just for the pure spiteful fun of it. And then he'll rip your throat out, and enjoy it twice as much for having first tricked you into trusting him.*

Alys swallowed another lump of stew. *No,* she told herself, *I'll take his help, but if it comes to that, I'll kill him before he kills me. He's just a—IT's just a—dragon. It's not a real person.*

She took another swallow. Even if she was

in too much turmoil to taste anything, the food would keep her from starving. It would give her the strength she would need later. She said, "Have you considered what we talked about yesterday?"

Selendrile finally shifted position and sat on the floor, but still said nothing.

"About a plan?" she prompted.

"It's your revenge," he pointed out. "Surely you don't expect me to tell you what to do."

That was exactly what she'd expected.

Alys sighed. "Do you have any suggestions?"

She thought she caught a flicker of what may have been disappointment on his face. "You want to do Gower last," he reminded her.

"Yes."

"Then it would seem to make sense to do his family directly before him."

"So Atherton first, since he's in Griswold?"

The dragon-youth inclined his head.

"What exactly are we going to do to him?"

Selendrile only continued to watch her.

Alys shook her head. It was one thing to know she wanted Atherton to pay for what he'd done to her and her father; it was quite another to come up with a plan. "Maybe I shouldn't rush into this. We can go to Griswold, see what the town is like, decide on what to do there."

Selendrile asked, "Where do humans live when they're in a town they don't know, while they're trying to decide what to do?"

"An inn, I guess," Alys said. "If they have gold or silver to pay."

Selendrile smiled, faint and chilly, and Alys shivered.

His amusement shifted to something darker, a mood for which she had no name. "I think," he told her, "you'll have to go as a boy."

"What?" she squeaked. "I'd never pa—"

"For your own protection," he interrupted. "The other choice is to go as a married couple, though that has the disadvantage of Atherton recognizing you as soon as he sees you."

Alys found it hard to catch a breath despite the knowledge that he was watching her and was aware of her every movement. *A married couple?*

He took her silence as agreement. "We'll go as brothers. Pick a name."

Alys clenched her teeth, knowing that he was right, that a woman couldn't take a room by herself at a respectable inn, that he didn't need to bring her all the way to Griswold if he intended her harm. Still—soft-spoken and almost tame as he seemed at the moment—she could never be *sure* what he was thinking, could never trust him completely. She could never allow herself to forget that one of them would most probably end up killing the other. "Jocko," she said, picking the name out of the air.

Selendrile turned his back to her and, sitting cross-legged, gathered up his long fair hair at the nape of his neck. "If you can braid this or tie it up somehow to look more in the fashion of your countrymen, we'll attract less attention."

There was no chance Selendrile would *ever* not attract attention. Or was this another twist in the game, offering up trust—or the semblance of it—by turning his back to her while she sat in a kitchen full of knives?

Alys picked up the piece of twine that had tied the apple sack, and then, to shake him, to reveal as a lie his pose of complacent indifference, she reached for one of the knives. But he didn't scramble to his feet, or tense up, or give any indication that he was even aware that she held a weapon. The knife was badly made, wobbling in its wooden handle, but she managed to saw the twine into manageable lengths, watching him all the while. Not foolhardy, after all, but only unobservant. Still holding the knife, she approached his unprotected back, knowing this was stupid, that he could whirl around at the last moment with that deadly speed of his and turn the blade on her, and she would never have the chance to protest it had only been a test.

Alys knelt behind him. And only then made the decision that it *was* a test. She'd do his hair, and then afterward show him the knife she'd silently laid on the floor, show him the danger he'd never known he was in.

Alys ran her fingers through his hair to separate it into strands for braiding. When she was finished, she pulled the braids back and fastened them behind. "There," she said.

Selendrile turned before she had a chance to pick up the knife, but his purple eyes locked onto hers, never glancing to either side or down to the floor. "Turn around," he told her.

"Why?"

"So I can cut off your hair." With his eyes

never flickering away from hers, he picked up the knife she had finally convinced herself he couldn't have seen.

She stiffened. "Why can't we just braid it like yours?"

"Because there can't be a hint of a question in anybody's mind. The moment someone suspects you're a girl, the clothes won't work. You don't want Atherton to recognize you right away. You want him to feel there's something familiar about you so that he thinks about you after you're gone, after you've destroyed him. You want him to realize who you are only when you're not there anymore."

"That's what I want, is it?" she asked, unable to look away from the blade in his hand.

He used the knife to indicate she put her back to him, to take her turn in this game of trust and nerve.

She sat down, and he swept her hair back over her shoulders. His fingers were light and gentle as they brushed against her cheek, her neck. But the knife tugged mercilessly as he hacked away long strands of hair.

It'll grow back, she thought as big chunks of

it dropped all around her. And even if it didn't, this would still be worth it, to get revenge on Atherton. And then Una and Etta, Gower's family. And then Gower himself.

Anything would be worth that.

Chapter 6

ALYS ASSUMED THAT they would set out for Griswold immediately, so she was surprised when—after she thought they were all set— Selendrile said, "Wait here."

"For what?"

"You said we'd need gold and silver."

"Ah," Alys said, "of which you have..."

He gave a perfectly charming smile. "Much."

"Much." Alys sighed. "I can imagine. Wouldn't it be faster if I went with you?"

He shook his head.

"Once it's really dark, they'll close and lock the town gates."

Again he shook his head.

"You don't trust me," she said.

He just smiled.

By the time he came back, clutching a leather bag of coins, and by the time she rebraided his hair and by the time they'd walked to Griswold, the sky had turned from gray to black. Now here they were, standing with only the moon to light them, trying to convince the night watch that they were, in fact, harmless and should be allowed to enter.

The guard who had the lantern leaned down from his vantage on top of the wall, holding the light out to get a better look at them. But since he was up about eight feet higher than they were, they got a better look at him than he got at them.

Alys thought he looked cranky and suspicious.

The other guard seemed to be the first man's superior; the one with the lantern had fetched him when Alys and Selendrile had knocked on the wooden gate, demanding entrance and refusing to go away and come back in the morning. Alys couldn't see him, but he *sounded* cranky and suspicious. He said, "How do we know you ain't that witch?"

Selendrile, who'd been looking down to

avoid the glare of the light in his eyes, jerked his head up, but appeared more amused than startled.

Word of her couldn't have traveled this far this fast, could it? "What witch?" Alys asked.

"That old witch lives behind one of them waterfalls up to the glen." The guard jerked his head in the general direction of the mountain.

Alys realized she'd been holding her breath. She shook her head to indicate she didn't know what he was talking about.

"Sold her soul to the devil for the witch-power," he explained. "And never did use it for nothing but mischief and sorrow all her life. But now she's old and close to dying, she's looking to buy someone else's soul to take her place. Been bothering decent, law-abiding folk."

Alys continued to shake her head.

Selendrile finally spoke up. "No witches here," he said in a tone that gave away the fact that he was suspiciously close to laughing.

Alys added: "Does either of us look like an old witch?"

The guards were unimpressed with irony or logic. "Gate opens at dawn. Come back then."

If she weren't disguised as a boy in tunic,

breeches, and cap, she could have started crying, loudly, to see if that would help, but under the circumstances it probably wouldn't. The first guard straightened, pulling the lantern up with him. Seeing the light move away, Alys yelled up, "It was the dragon's fault." She was aware of Selendrile watching her, but she was watching the light. It stopped moving, returned to the wall.

"Dragon?" the guard said.

Alys decided to put a little quiver into her voice after all. "It killed our parents, ravaged our fields. We didn't dare stay another night. We were afraid it might come back." She pointed vaguely in the direction from which they'd come, then snuffled loudly, rubbing her sleeve arm over her nose.

The guard's voice became more gentle. "How old are you lads?"

"Twelve," she said, because there was no way she could pass as a fifteen-year-old boy and because she figured the younger the guards thought them, the more sympathetic they would be. Then, indicating Selendrile, she said, "And seventeen," which was what he looked like. *Seventeen, going on three hundred.*

The guards muttered together.

"All right," the senior one finally said.

There was another delay, then the creak of rope and wood as the latch was raised, and the gate swung open.

The guard stood in the middle of the open space, glowering at them over his crossbow sights.

Alys forced down a swallow.

"Move, move," he told them from between clenched teeth.

Selendrile gave her a shove just strong enough that she staggered forward a couple of paces. Her first thought was that he was offering her up as the target, but he came with her, and the guard continued to aim at the spot where they *had* stood, all the while anxiously peering into the shadows beyond the walls.

The heavy gate thudded back into place, maneuvered by the guard who'd been holding the lantern. Once the latch was secured, the other lowered his crossbow, apparently satisfied that no one was coming in with them. A lot of good gate or wall would do to keep Selendrile or his real kin out.

"You got people in Griswold?" the guard asked.

"No," Alys said. "But we do have a few copper pieces for lodging." She wanted him to know they weren't going to make a nuisance of themselves begging, without indicating they had enough that it'd be worth his while to rob them.

But now that she and Selendrile were in, the guards lost interest. The first was already scrambling up to resume his position on the wall. "The Green Barrel's probably your best bet, then," the other said, waving airily in an arc that indicated three-fourths of the town. "There's probably cleaner and definitely cheaper, but at least you won't wake up in the morning to find your throats slit."

While Alys paused to sort that out, Selendrile took her arm and started pulling her in the general direction the guard had indicated.

The inhabitants of Saint Toby's would be mostly home and in bed by this hour, but Griswold was a lot bigger, if no grander, and there were still lights on in many of the buildings and people out on the streets. For Alys it was a strange sensation, being in a town big enough to get lost in, being surrounded by people she hadn't known all her life. By the time she and

Selendrile finally found themselves in front of the Green Barrel Inn, her heart was beating too hard and fast for her to ask Selendrile to wait while she caught her breath.

He swept her past the painted rain barrel that gave the place its name and in through the open front door.

This is where we get set upon by thieves and cutthroats, Alys thought, *just waiting for an innocent victim to blunder in.* Unless, of course, anybody took more than the hastiest glance at Selendrile, in which case they were sure to see beyond his human disguise to the monster beneath, and that would start a commotion of a different sort.

But nobody at the dozen or so tables in the place looked at them with anything that even the wary Alys could call more than indifferent curiosity. From across the room came a skinny little man who was no taller than Alys, wiping his hands on his apron and smiling. His gaze flickered from Alys to Selendrile and he looked neither murderous nor about to panic. "May I help you?" he asked instead. Asked Selendrile, who appeared the older.

How can he look at him and not see? Alys

wondered. She said: "My brother and I, we're looking for a room."

The innkeeper shifted his gaze back to her and raised his brows skeptically.

"Our parents were killed in a dragon raid," she said. "It knocked down our house, burned our fields. We've come to Griswold looking for work."

One of the people at the nearest table asked, "You Upton's boys then?"

It was too dangerous; if somebody here knew this man Upton, somebody else might know his sons. "No," Alys admitted. "We're from the other side of Saint Toby's village. But there wasn't any work to be had there. We've got enough money for the night"—Selendrile had brought enough money to buy the place, but she certainly wasn't going to announce that—"or we could work for our keep."

The innkeeper hesitated and Alys nudged Selendrile. The gold was useless—there was no way a pair of orphaned peasants could come by gold—but she'd had him put a few of the silver and copper pieces in his pocket. Now he took one of these out and held it to the innkeeper.

"This'll get you your lodgings and a bit of

supper if you haven't eaten yet," the man said. "Breakfast comes with the room. Odelia," he called to a girl who was cleaning one of the tables. She looked just like him except for the fact that she had more hair and was obviously a couple of years younger than Alys. "You and your sister get a room set up."

"This way, please," the little girl said. She led them through the kitchen, where she introduced them as paying customers to another girl. This older one put down the spoon she was using to stir a kettle of soup and gave Selendrile a long, studied stare.

Here it comes, Alys thought.

With admirable calm, the older sister said, "We need to get straw for the bedding." She flung her arm around her sister's shoulders, but Alys saw her fingers dig into Odelia's upper arm, and the younger girl's confused expression as her sister hustled her outdoors. *Run, run,* every instinct warned Alys. *They're going to raise an alarm.* Selendrile was looking around the kitchen, oblivious to it all, peeking into the corners, looking under the counters. "We've got to get out of here," Alys warned him in a frantic whisper.

"We just got here," Selendrile pointed out, picking up a clay pot lid as though he'd never seen one before.

The two girls returned, carrying armloads of straw. Alys caught the hurried glance Odelia gave Selendrile before she lowered her gaze. "This way," she murmured.

But that wasn't fear which was causing her cheeks to redden. Alys glanced at the older sister, who was staring at Selendrile again.

Oh, heaven help me—they're flirting with him, she realized.

The two sisters led them to an upstairs room and began stuffing the straw into the mattress.

Alys tugged on Selendrile's arm. "There's only one sleeping pallet," she hissed at him.

He'd been looking out the window at the people in the street below, and he turned to her with a blank expression that could have been either lack of understanding or his usual give-nothing expression.

"What's that?" the older girl asked, straightening.

"There's only one sleeping pallet," Alys repeated.

"There's hardly room for two."

"Yes," Alys said, finding her patience wearing thin at the smug tone, "but there are two of us."

"But this one's wide enough for two," said the younger girl, Odelia, "and you *are* brothers." Both girls seemed on the verge of a giggling fit.

"Of course we're brothers"—Alys was balanced between annoyance and panic—"but we need two sleeping pallets."

Selendrile came up behind her and flung his arm around her shoulders in imitation of the older sister's protective gesture. Somehow Alys kept from jumping out of her skin. Selendrile told the girls, "My brother kicks and snores terribly."

This time the girls did burst out laughing, but, leaving, they promised to bring up more bedding.

Alys sat on the sleeping pallet and rested her head in her hands and waited for the thudding of her heart to slow down. "I think I'll stay here until I've calmed back down," she muttered between her fingers. "Barricade the door for a year or two, will you?"

Selendrile stooped down beside her, his leg

brushing against her arm. This time Alys *did* jump. But there was no way to move back to put more distance between them, not without scrambling over the mattress. "Staying in the room makes no sense," he said. "We've got to go out and mingle with the townspeople."

Alys sighed.

The worst part of it was knowing he was right.

Chapter 7

THE THING WAS, Alys thought, Selendrile made a passable human.

No, that was being unfairly snide.

He made a very good human.

At first, when they'd just come down into the inn's common room, she had been able to watch him watching others, his responses a half-heartbeat too slow as he gauged others' reactions. Made judgments. Learned. Soon he no longer glanced at her to see what emotions his expression should indicate. He didn't wait for her to answer when somebody asked him a question. It was together that they wove their story of how their farm had been destroyed by a dragon and how, with no family surviving, they had made their way to Griswold. When somebody asked why they hadn't gone to Saint Toby's, which was closer, Alys gave the same answer she had to the guards, "No work," but Selendrile added, "Well, that and..." And he let his voice drift off, so that everybody looked at Alys, as the more talkative brother, to finish the thought.

"That and...," Alys repeated, wondering what, if anything, Selendrile had in mind. He sat chin in hand, elbow on table, and in the flickering light of candles and hearth, his purple eyes appeared soft and gentle though she knew they were really hard and cold. She had taken note of the way the women in the room watched him, as though pretty eyes and a sweet smile were any indication of what a person was. She decided he *didn't* have anything in mind but was only trying to make things more difficult in order to watch her squirm. "Saint Toby's is not a nice place," she said with a sigh, which seemed to her to be appropriately vague and totally dull, but suddenly everyone, even Odelia's older sister, was waiting for her next words.

Alys rolled the cup of ale that had come with their dinner between her palms. Didn't anyone notice that Selendrile hadn't taken a bite of his meal, had never once sipped from his cup? "The thing is—"

"And this is very hard to talk about...," Selendrile interrupted, which might have passed among the listeners as explanation for her hesitation, but put her no closer to what to say.

Still, she looked at him appraisingly. If he wasn't determined to see her make a fool of herself, what was he up to? Alys realized she'd been so intent on explaining themselves, on fitting in, that she'd come close to losing sight of their purpose here. Explaining how Atherton had falsely condemned her would do no good. The people here had no more reason to believe her than her own townsfolk, especially if they'd been recently harassed by a witch of their own. On the other hand, if she couldn't get the Inquisitor in trouble by accusing him of what he'd done, she might get him in trouble by accusing him of something he hadn't done. "The thing is," she said, "someone stole things from the chapel in Saint Toby's."

It seemed to her that stealing from the Church had to be the worst of crimes, and from the expressions of the people around her, they agreed. Except for Selendrile. She couldn't tell what he thought.

"The poor box was ripped out of the wall," she continued, "the silver candlesticks snatched right off the altar."

"Who would do such a thing?" someone asked in a voice of awed horror.

"Inquisitor Atherton—"

Selendrile gave her a swift kick under the table. While Alys tried to be unobtrusive about rubbing her ankle, he said, "Inquisitor Atherton came to Saint Toby's to see about some girl who was accused of witchcraft."

"Not," Alys stressed, "that there was any real—"

Selendrile sat abruptly back in his chair, dragging his hands across the table so that he struck his cup and sent it spinning into her lap. "Sorry," he said blandly as she jumped to her feet and wiped ineffectively at the wetness.

And what was that look supposed to mean?

"Anyway," he finished her story for her, "what with all the commotion of the theft and the witch trial, nobody from Saint Toby's was in a hospitable mood. We were rushed out of there so fast we didn't have a chance to tell them about the dragon. And then, coming here, we had no way of knowing if we'd left the thieves behind us in Saint Toby's or if they were about to waylay us on the road."

One of the townsmen shook his head. "Leave it to Atherton to get caught up in a witch trial while thieves are happily stealing the shirt off your back."

This seemed a fine opening to Alys, but Selendrile tipped his head at her the way he'd first done when he'd been in dragon shape. "My brother and I have had a very long, hard day." His voice had just the right edge of weariness to it so that Alys could have sworn that he'd just lost his parents and everything he had in the world in the past two days.

The crowd parted for them, though Alys could hear the background murmur of people saying, "Terrible thing," and "What's the world coming to?"

She waited until they were back up in their room before turning on him. "What was that for?" she demanded, hands on wet hips and aware of how she stank of ale.

He flashed one of his colder smiles. "I didn't want you accusing him."

"I thought that was the whole point."

"Better to play naive and let people draw their own conclusions." He held his arms out straight and slowly turned.

Checking to see if the room was big enough for him to resume dragon shape, she realized. It wasn't. Which was probably a good thing; she doubted the floor would have held his weight.

He sat down on one of the sleeping pallets and looked up at her as he took off his boots. "What do people say when they're about to go to sleep together?"

"We are *not* about to go to sleep together," she informed him in a voice that was too loud, suddenly aware of how close the narrow room forced the two pallets to be.

"Well, I'm planning to go to sleep." He took off his shirt. "Of course, you're welcome to stay awake if you choose."

"Stay away from me," she warned, as furious as afraid. "Just stay over there away from me."

He managed the same innocent look he'd done downstairs for the women of Griswold.

But she knew better.

She turned her back so she wouldn't have to

look at him and lay down in her damp, smelly clothes, as close to the far wall as she could get. "They say 'good night,'" she told him.

But he was too busy laughing to answer.

IT WAS MIDDAY when Alys woke up, and Selendrile was gone. *Wonderful*, she grumbled to herself, and went downstairs without waiting for him.

Her meal was the same as last night, except this time the soup was served cold and the bread warm. "So where's that handsome brother of yours?" asked the woman who was working in the kitchen. *The mother of the two girls?* Alys wondered, unable to decide whether the woman had been one of those present last night, or whether Selendrile's reputation had already begun to spread.

Alys shrugged and took her bowl out into the common room. Only a few people were here this early. She recognized a couple of faces, and smiled and nodded back at the greetings she got, but chose a table by herself.

What am I doing? she asked herself. She couldn't just continue to blunder around, hoping that things would fall into place and that

Selendrile would pull through and help her when she needed it. She forced herself to think of Atherton—though her mind had a tendency to shy away from the turmoil of angry feelings he stirred up. Assuming the best about him, he might have been unaware that Gower and his family were lying to get her father's shop and land. Assuming the best, he might have been so eager to solve Griswold's dragon problem that when he'd found a maiden to offer to the dragon he hadn't cared.

Alys tried to focus her feelings of rage. All right. She and Selendrile had made up their own lies, had said that someone had stolen from the little chapel in Saint Toby's at just the time Inquisitor Atherton had been there. Would the people of Griswold draw the conclusion that Atherton himself had been the thief? Possible, she decided, but not definite. Would they believe it if she and Selendrile could get some of Selendrile's gold into Atherton's possession? She thought back to the faces of the townsfolk last night, when she had first mentioned the Inquisitor's name. She hadn't been concentrating, because Selendrile had been attacking her with foot and ale. Still, she didn't think she'd seen any smiles, any softening of their expressions the way she'd have seen if somebody had mentioned Father Joseph's name in Saint Toby's. And at least one in their audience had complained about Atherton's preoccupation with witch trials. Surely he couldn't be popular. Not with his high-handed manner and the amount of satisfaction he obviously got from condemning people to death. She remembered the large gemmed crucifix that would be as showy and out of place in this town of simple homespun and rough-carved furniture as it had been in her own village. Surely the people here must resent him, and surely resentment was the first step toward convicting him.

The second step was hers.

The second step was confronting Atherton.

Chapter 8

ATHERTON'S HOUSE was behind the church, off the main street. Alys knocked, knowing that if he wasn't home, her plans would be delayed even more, but the idea of seeing him again— of letting him see her—was almost enough to send her back to the Green Barrel to wait for Selendrile. She braced herself, but still wasn't prepared.

The Inquisitor himself flung open the door without her having heard footsteps approach. "What is it?" he asked, standing close enough to spit on. He hadn't changed at all. Which, after two days, shouldn't have surprised her. But the knowledge that he had condemned an innocent victim to be devoured had left no physical trace on his face. His pale brown eyes regarded her coldly. Surely she hadn't changed either, and he would see through her silly disguise.

She tugged her cap lower over her forehead. "I...I..."

"What is it?" he repeated, patience gone in the span of two stammers.

He didn't know her after all. Her plan, such as it was, was safe. So far. It wasn't much to go on, but it was all she had.

She found speaking easier if she didn't look at him, and she lowered her gaze to the dusty street. "I come from Tierbo," she said, trying to match the regional accent to disguise her voice. "There's a man there what got himself possessed. Done speak in voices, he does, and throw fits. He got a gleam in his right eye what ain't normal and his left eye's all clouded over and turned up in his head like. My da says, 'Better get the priest,' he says, 'before somebody gets hurt.' Will ya come?"

"Tierbo," Atherton repeated. It was a seaport, a good three days away.

"My da says give this to you, for your church here." She reached into the bag of silver Selendrile had brought and grabbed a fistful of the coins. When she looked up from handing it over, she knew she had him. "There be more," she said, "what they were still collecting when I left."

Atherton nodded slowly. "Tonight's the vigil of Saint Emmett, Griswold's patron saint. Be here first thing tomorrow morning, and look you don't keep me waiting."

Now that she had started, Alys wasn't willing to delay. She saw Atherton start to move his arm—he had it up against the doorway as though to block her lest she try to forge ahead into his room. In another moment he would slam the door shut, dismissing her. She said, "Right, that's what my da said."

She watched him weigh his choices. He tightened his grip on the door, but asked, "*What* did he say?"

"Not to keep him waiting. He's in a terrible rush, the possessed man's that violent. That's why Da sent my brother over to Wendbury, to ask the priest there to come, too—see?— figurin' someone's got to get there first." The implication she hoped he'd come away with was that only the first would get the extra money.

Atherton considered. Then, as though doing her a favor, "All right, all right," he said. "If the man's that bad off, we'll set out tonight. Meet me here directly after the vigil service." Alys was nodding, but he repeated, "Directly. I'll have my things packed and a horse ready to go, and I want no nonsense from you."

"No nonsense," Alys agreed.

Atherton looked doubtful, but he said nothing more. He just—finally—slammed the door in her face.

ALYS SPENT THE REST of the afternoon wandering about the town of Griswold, hoping to find Selendrile and meanwhile talking to the merchants about what work was available, lest anyone become suspicious. Nobody had seen Selendrile since last night, but she did get three job offers.

As evening set in, her mood shifted from annoyance to anger to worry.

Then, as she passed a dark, narrow alleyway, she heard someone say, *"Psst."*

Hoping that it had nothing to do with her, Alys ducked her head and walked faster.

"Psst! Little boy."

Alys glanced into the darkness only long

enough to see that there were far too many shadows. But apparently that was long enough. She heard a quick, startled laugh. Then the voice—a woman's—called, "Little girl disguised as a boy."

It was no use pretending she didn't hear or that it wasn't true. From the corner of the alley with the darkest shadows she caught a movement—a gnarled white hand beckoning. Alys looked around to make sure nobody on the street was watching and stepped into the alley.

Part of the shadows resolved themselves into the shape of an old woman with a shawl over her head. "Well, well, my sweet one," the woman said. But despite her gentle words, Alys flinched when she raised her hand to brush Alys's cheek. "What's such a pretty child doing dressed in nasty boys' clothes and with her lovely hair all cut off? Are you in trouble?" The woman smiled gleefully. "You *are*." She tapped the side of her own nose with a crooked finger. "I can *smell* people in trouble. You've gone and gotten yourself in bad company, haven't you?"

Not as bad as this, Alys wanted to say, but the words caught in her throat, and Alys was afraid that might be because they were untrue. She took a step away and felt the rough wall at her back, snagging her clothes and hair.

"You better get out," the old woman warned, "before you get in too deep."

"Yes," Alys said, easing toward the mouth of the alley, toward the open street. "Thank you for your advice."

"Advice is free," the woman said. "Would you like my help?"

Alys shook her head and the woman laughed. Alys felt the edge of the corner building, realized she was back on the street. Was the woman going to follow her? Prevent her from leaving? Yell out the truth about Alys to all the world?

But the woman did nothing, yelled nothing, only continued to laugh. "I'll be here if you change your mind," she called after Alys. "Here or in the glen behind the waterfall. I may well be your only chance—if you don't wait too long."

Alys ran the rest of the way back to the Green Barrel Inn, but she didn't go there directly, just in case she was being followed. She ran past it and circled to the right, then the left, temporarily lost herself, and only then approached the inn. At the door she stopped and looked back.

Silly, she told herself for the nagging feeling that the witch was watching her from the evening darkness. The witch was too old to run, and besides, Alys would have heard her. Still, it was a relief to enter the Green Barrel's brightly lit common room, especially when she saw Selendrile. He was sitting at a table by the fire, where the flames cast their glow on the long blond hair he'd gathered at the nape of his neck. For a moment she forgot how annoyed she was at him, until she noticed his impatient look, as though *he'd* spent all afternoon looking for *her.*

Which she didn't believe for a moment.

She sat down next to him before speaking so that not everybody in the room would overhear their business. "Where have you been?" she demanded.

He smiled, as though to say she didn't really want to know.

Which she didn't. "Don't do that again. I was worried."

"About me?" His tone was insincere, which made her answer: "About the plan," though she hadn't liked the thought he could be hurt or in trouble. He sat back on the bench and smiled. "What about the plan?" he asked.

She couldn't answer, because the cook came out then, carrying bowls of smoked-mutton stew, which she set before them on the table.

"None for me, thank you," Selendrile said, never looking at her.

"You don't eat enough," the cook scolded him, "that's your problem."

At which point he did look at her.

Any appetite that Alys may have had dissolved in that look. "Let's go to our room," she said, scrambling to get to her feet, to get away. "Come on, Selendrile."

He got up slowly, with a smile for the cook, which she no doubt took as charming.

In their room, Alys talked fast to get his mind away from the path she was sure it was taking. "I went to see Atherton," she said, and saw a shadow of surprise. "I told him I was from Tierbo and that we needed him there for an exorcism. He agreed to come. I'm supposed to meet him after the vigil service tonight to take him there."

"When is a vigil service?" he asked.

She suddenly wondered if he knew *what* a

vigil service was. Or an exorcism, for that matter. "Sundown. Which means it already started, so we'll have to hurry. My plan, since you weren't there to help, was to put the rest of the gold that you brought into his saddlebags, and then somehow get people to notice. I hoped that they'd think he'd been stealing from them, maybe." It sounded so lame, so ridiculous.

Instead of saying that, he pulled a large leather bag out from under his bedding.

So that's what he'd been doing, at least part of the day. It was more gold, much more. He'd also brought a pair of silver candlesticks, a delicately engraved silver goblet studded with emeralds, and a little golden plate—which, if it wasn't a paten meant to hold the Eucharist during Mass, certainly could pass as one. She tried not to gawk like a peasant at court, but judging from his half smile she hadn't quite pulled it off. "I take it these are from your . . . ah . . ."

"Hoard."

". . . hoard," she repeated, wondering why she felt guilty saying it if he didn't. "Good." *Good?* He'd stolen these things, how could she be saying "good" about that? "I can put part of this in his saddlebags and then make a little slit,

93

so some of it spills out on the street while every-body's watching him leave for Tierbo. I saw that his house has a small upper window. I couldn't fit through, but if you could get in and hide the rest of this in Atherton's room, it'll seem as though he's been stealing for a long time."

He nodded, following her reasoning. "If you can toss the bag up into the room, I can turn into a bird, fly in the window, change back to human, hide the things, resume bird shape..." He considered. "Of course, if I walk into the church without any clothes, somebody's sure to notice. *You* always do."

Alys felt her cheeks get warm.

Selendrile smiled that dragon smile, which always made her afraid she was missing something obvious.

She said, "I'll bring your clothes and hide them behind the church. Join me as soon as you can."

He nodded and Alys tried to think if they were forgetting anything. "All right," she said slowly. She put her back to him before he could get his shirt up over his head.

Chapter 9

LIGHT FROM THE CANDLES streamed out of the church windows into the street behind the church, where Alys stood in the shadows. Anybody watching would be able to see her clearly, and the only thing that gave her the courage to step out of the shadows was the knowledge that the streets were nearly deserted—just about all the townspeople would be at the vigil service.

A huge black shadow flapped against a nearby wall, silent warning that someone was approaching.

The witch, Alys thought, realizing at the same moment that there was no place to hide the two sacks of gold she was holding. The witch had *said* she could smell people in trouble, and of course she wouldn't be at the service. Too late, Alys realized she had been so intent on telling Selendrile about the Inquisitor, she hadn't mentioned the witch at all.

But it was a trick of candlelight and nerves. The shadow got smaller and smaller, and where shadow was finally met by substance, it was only a raven that had nearly caused her to panic. Selendrile: She could tell by the way he cocked his head at her. He had settled on one of the church's gargoyle waterspouts, which just went to show how useful those figures were at protecting the building from evil spirits.

Grimly Alys moved beneath the window of Atherton's house. What if he'd closed the shutters against the night air?

But he hadn't.

Taking a deep breath, she flung the sack full of money.

It struck the wall not even halfway up and fell to the ground with a clunk and a jangle.

Alys kept her back to the raven, sure that Selendrile would find a way to look superior and smug, even in bird form. She retrieved the bag, threw it again. Missed again. She hoped the service was a nice long one. How would she explain herself, standing in the dark, hurling a bagful of money at the Inquisitor's wall? For that matter, what would she do if the bag burst open and scattered coins all over the street?

Atherton's horse was nearby, readied and tethered, brought earlier by one of the boys from the public stable so that Atherton could leave immediately after the service. Alys had the sinking sensation that she'd never get to that part of the plan. The horse watched her and the raven warily.

On the fifth try, Alys got the sack through the window, and Selendrile dove in after it.

Gingerly, Alys approached the horse. "Easy, easy," she whispered, though it had already calmed down now that Selendrile was indoors. She got the silver candlesticks out of her own sack, then pulled everything out of the Inquisitor's saddlebags. Using one of the candlesticks, she poked a hole through the leather at the seam, then repacked the bag, starting with handfuls of gold.

With the coins in there, not all of the Inquisitor's clothes would fit. Now what? She pushed damp hair off her sweaty forehead and forced herself to remain calm. Selendrile wasn't here to give her advice, so she'd better come up with a plan on her own. She set aside a bulky cape and managed to jam in the rest. Giving the horse one final pat, she scooped up both the bundle of Selendrile's clothes and Atherton's cloak. The first she left against the back wall of the church, as planned, the other in the wooden poor box just inside the front door.

The vigil service was almost over. She arrived just in time for the final benediction. Moments later, Selendrile slipped in beside her, and there was a murmur of disapproval from the surrounding people.

Oh no, she thought, assuming the townsfolk were upset because she had come in late and Selendrile had not quite made it at all. She opened her mouth to apologize, but already others had started talking—whispering, because of the place, but very intense, very upset.

"What happened?" at least three different voices asked. But nobody was even looking at her for an explanation. She heard Saint Emmett's name mentioned, and the word "relic," and the fact that Father Donato and Inquisitor Atherton had been as obviously surprised as everybody else. There were two priests in Griswold, Alys surmised, since Inquisitor Atherton was called away so often to deal with witches and dragons and demons, and somebody had to carry on the daily routine. But the single word she heard most often was "gone."

Trying to make sense of the jumble of voices, she let herself be carried along with the flow of people leaving the church, though it separated her from Selendrile. "Excuse me," she said at a point where only two people were talking at the same time, "something's missing?"

Closest to her was a man about her father's age and build, a cloth merchant who just this afternoon had offered to hire her to clean his shop and run errands. "That's right," he said, "you're new here and wouldn't know. The chalice is gone—the one Saint Emmett brought back from his pilgrimage to the Holy Land."

"They had to do the service without a chalice?" Alys asked.

"It was a gift to Saint Emmett from the bishop of Jerusalem," somebody explained. And somebody else: "Father Donato only uses it on special occasions on account of it's a relic, and because it's so precious since it's made of silver and emeralds."

On the verge of expressing her sympathy,

Alys felt the words drain out of her. Silver and emeralds?

"Oh my," said Selendrile, suddenly right beside her. "Then it's not likely to have been mislaid."

Alys was ready to strangle him for not having told her when he'd had the chance. How *could* he have taken the risk of stealing Griswold's chalice right out from under everybody's noses? But apparently the townsfolk read her furious expression as shock and dismay, for nobody asked her what was wrong.

Selendrile looked at her calmly and evenly, then raised his eyebrows expectantly.

Then, with an expression of chagrin since she was obviously not jumping in and playing her part as he expected, he said, "Just like at Saint Toby's."

The murmur of voices intensified. Was everyone who'd been in the church crowded around them in the square?

Slowly and deliberately Selendrile said, "Maybe it wasn't somebody from Saint Toby's who stole those candlesticks after all. There must be a thief going from town to town stealing from churches. We *were* lucky not to get set upon on the road. Did anyone see any strangers loitering about the church?"

In Alys's opinion he'd gone and convicted them. But nobody pointed out that *they* were strangers. "Maybe," Alys said, sure that the crime was written plain on her face, "we should tell Father Donato and Inquisitor Atherton that there was a similar theft at Saint Toby's church."

The crowd surged around the corner toward Atherton's house. Atherton was standing outside, one hand on the tether of his readied mount. Straightaway, Alys's gaze went to the saddlebag. If she'd made the hole too large, people would see that it had been made intentionally. If she'd made it too small, the coins wouldn't fall through and all that she'd have accomplished would have been to enrich her enemy. She forced herself to look away from the bag and now saw that Father Donato was out here, too. By the look of them, he and Inquisitor Atherton had been arguing.

Selendrile caught her arm as though the crowd's jostling had caused him to lose his balance, but Alys had been looking at him and knew that wasn't the case. "Stay back," he hissed into her ear. He made his way forward as

Atherton cast an annoyed glance at all the noisy people.

"Quiet!" the Inquisitor bellowed.

The townspeople stilled, so Alys could hear Father Donato say in his thin and whiny voice, "But why *must* you go now, when the church has been burglarized and we don't know how, and the villains might strike again?"

Atherton was aware of how many waited for his answer. "I already told you, I'm urgently needed in Tierbo for an exorcism."

"But surely tomorrow is soon en—"

"The boy they sent said it couldn't wait. In fact, he's supposed to be here now"—Alys ducked to avoid the searching gaze that passed over the crowd—"and if he doesn't hurry, I may be forced to leave without him. As for the burglar, just put three trustworthy men inside the church, lock the doors, then post three more men outside. I'm confident you can handle everything until I return."

Alys wasn't confident Father Donato could handle anything. He seemed a mild little man on the verge of being overwhelmed by life.

By this time, Selendrile had made it to the

edge of the crowd. People were calling out to Atherton, telling him about the theft of the silver candlesticks from Saint Toby's church, urging Selendrile to step forward and speak up, demanding attention in a confusion of voices that even Alys, knowing what they were saying, couldn't sort out.

Atherton's horse became suddenly skittish. It snorted and sidestepped and threw its head back in wide-eyed terror. Alys recognized that reaction from the cart horses that had brought her to the hill where she'd been staked out as dragon's bait. She glanced again at the saddlebag. The horse was shying away from Selendrile, but since the dragon-youth stood so close to everybody else, anyone would have assumed the size and noise of the crowd was the problem.

Atherton dragged on the bridle but to no effect. Finally he said, "I've got to get away before this foul beast steps on someone. Just set up guards to watch the church, and guards to watch the guards, and I'll be back as soon as I can." He swung up into the saddle and dragged hard to the right, which was toward the crowd in the street, which was exactly where the horse didn't want to go. The horse reared, then landed back on all fours with what was probably bone-jarring force.

Alys, who was looking for it, saw a coin fall to the packed earth.

As Atherton guided the horse into the street, Selendrile swooped in and picked up the coin. "Inquisitor," he called.

The horse reared again, and the saddlebag lost another coin. Atherton craned around to see what was the matter.

"You dropped this." Selendrile held up the coin so that it sparkled goldenly in the light of the nearby torches.

"Not mine," Atherton said, obviously annoyed with the interruption, the horse, and the world.

"Not mine either," Selendrile said. He held the coin up as though to let its owner claim it.

"There's another one." Alys pointed. "Under the horse."

Atherton's head swung round at the sound of her voice, and she stepped behind a wide woman lest he recognize her too early.

Someone else from the crowd retrieved the second coin.

"It's not mine," Atherton snapped when the man held it out to him. He sounded ill-tempered to have to admit it. "Now move out of my way. I have work to do."

Selendrile moved in closer. "Well, maybe you should hold it in safekeeping until the owner shows up."

At his approach, the horse reared again. This time several coins were jostled loose.

"They're coming from your saddlebag," someone pointed out.

"Nonsense," Atherton answered.

Another coin dropped onto the little pile, and the sound of it was clear in the silence that had settled over the crowd.

Father Donato came forward, wringing his hands in agitation. He licked his lips several times before he could bring himself to say what the townsfolk were already muttering amongst themselves. His voice was so soft, Alys could barely hear. "Perhaps we should take a look in that bag," he said, "just to . . . take a look."

Furious, Atherton swung off his horse. But as soon as he'd untied the bag and started to hand it to Father Donato, the entire bottom ripped out. Gold and silver coins poured onto the street, along with the silver candlesticks, the golden plate, and Saint Emmett's chalice.

"I—I—" Atherton moved from shock to suspicion in the interval between two breaths. "Somebody put these things here."

"Obviously," said the man who had tried to give Atherton the second coin. "Which just leaves us with the question of why you were so anxious to leave."

"Oh dear," Father Donato said, looking as though he were about to wring his hands off. "Oh dear, oh dear."

Atherton scowled. Although his words answered the townsman, he was looking at Father Donato. "I've been called to Tierbo for an exorcism, you silly little man."

"Tierbo's a seaport," someone pointed out. "Lots of smugglers, lots of opportunities to sell stolen goods."

"I did not steal these things," Atherton shouted.

"Oh dear, oh dear," Father Donato repeated.

Atherton grabbed him by the shoulders. "There was some boy, sent to call me to Tierbo.

That's where I'm going, and all we need to do is find him—"

That sounded like Alys's signal; she poked her head out from behind the wide lady.

"There!" Atherton cried. "There he is!"

Alys looked behind her and to both sides.

"You! You, boy!"

Alys stood there, as though waiting, like everybody else.

Atherton let go of Father Donato and pushed through the crowd to her. "Are you a simpleton, boy? I'm talking to you."

Again Alys looked to either side.

"Tell them about the man with the voices. Tell them that it wasn't my idea to go to Tierbo but that you summoned me."

"What?" Alys said.

He grabbed her by the front of her shirt, which she hadn't anticipated.

"Let go," she cried, twisting. The last thing she needed was for him to realize she was a girl. "I've never seen you before."

"You were here this afternoon!" Apparently he was too frantic to notice anything amiss. "Tell them you were here."

"The boy was with me," the cloth merchant said, "talking about working for me."

"He came to my shop, too," someone from behind called out.

"And mine." That person added, "And he sure don't come from Tierbo."

"Terrible thing," Father Donato said in his nervous little whisper-squeak, "terrible. Nothing like this has ever happened before. We'd better take a look in your rooms, Inquisitor Atherton."

"There's nothing amiss there," Atherton answered. Then he swung back to Alys and stuck his finger practically into her nose. Very quietly, very firmly, he said, "You were here."

"He can't have nothing to do with the thievin'," someone pointed out. "*He's* the one *told us* about the thievin'."

Two of the townsmen took Atherton by the arms and marched him back to his house, with Father Donato as the reluctant leader.

Too many people jammed into the house, so that Alys and Selendrile couldn't even see into the doorway, but it didn't take long before they heard someone cry out that there was a large leather bag full of gold in Atherton's clothes chest.

Selendrile motioned with his head for Alys to move away from all the people. At the next street, he turned to look back. "Well," he said, "what do you think? You don't look as pleased as I would have thought."

Alys had to stop to consider and realized she didn't feel as pleased as she would have thought. "I'm sorry Father Donato had to get involved," she said. "He seemed like a sweet man."

"Ah," Selendrile said.

She looked up at him sharply, trying to decide what that was supposed to mean.

"Maybe it'll be better with Gower," he said.

"Maybe," Alys agreed.

walls, higher than the trees, higher than the church steeple. At first she was disoriented, looking down on everything from the air, trying to make sense of half-familiar streets and buildings dimly lit by candles and torches and hearth fires, till her eyes began to cross and dizziness bubbled up in the space behind her eyes. *As soon as my stomach catches up to the rest of me, I'm going to be in serious trouble,* she thought.

But in another moment they'd left the town behind and were in the countryside and higher yet. Now the ground was too far away and too unreal to be frightening. Selendrile stretched his wings to catch an updraft, and fields and woods unrolled beneath them as he glided effortlessly on air currents. His grip around her waist was firm without being painful, and steady enough that she didn't worry about slipping loose. At the speed they were traveling, the rush of the wind past her ears was deafening. Still, by the time she saw that Selendrile was getting closer to the ground, she suddenly realized how disappointed she was at that thought. She laughed out loud at herself, and the sound was strange to her ears and, a moment later, was left miles behind.

With her feet once more on the ground,

Alys again found herself dizzy, but this time it was a giddy, pleasant sensation. She let Selendrile's clothes drop to the ground so that she could hold her arms out and spin around, with her face up to the stars, wishing she could hug them to herself. "That was wonderful!" she announced. "I love flying!"

She let herself fall to the ground and lay on her back watching the sky spin above her.

When things were finally standing still in their proper places again, she pointed up to a dark wisp of cloud shrouding the moon. "Next time"—she giggled—"if there is a next time—wouldn't it be fun to fly through a cloud—like diving into a big pile of unspun wool?"

Selendrile sat down beside her to pull on his boots. "You can't feel them."

Alys rolled over and propped herself up on an elbow. "What do you mean? Are they too high up for you to reach?"

He shook his head. "I can reach them. But they don't feel like anything. Well," he amended, "some of them are a bit damp. What's the second part of your plan?"

Slowly Alys sat up. The silhouettes of the hills to her left were suddenly familiar, and she realized Selendrile had brought them to land just a short walk from the village of Saint Toby's. She rubbed her chilled arms. "I don't think," she admitted, "I'll be able to use the same disguise as I did in Griswold. I've lived with these people all my life, and men's breeches and a hat aren't going to fool anybody."

"All right," Selendrile said equably.

She sat looking at him, and he sat looking at her.

"Well?" she finally asked.

He sighed. "Assuming we can work around people recognizing you, what would you like to see done?"

Alys considered. "Gower wanted my father's land so that he could expand his own shop. His wheelworking is very important to him. I think I'd like to see him lose his shop, ruin his reputation."

"Easy to do. What about the daughter?"

Alys remembered the glee with which Etta had embellished the false accusations her parents had made, and how she'd suggested burning Alys at the stake. She felt a tightness in her chest and was suddenly finding it difficult to breathe. "I want her to be accused of the same thing I was, to know that she's innocent and to have nobody believe her. I want her to be just as scared as I was."

Selendrile smiled. "And the mother?"

Alys jumped to her feet. "I don't know," she cried. "It's not going to work anyway. They'll recognize me as soon as they see me. Why are you doing this?"

The dragon-youth looked at her calmly, and whether he was considering the nature of clouds or thinking that he could have saved himself a lot of trouble by eating her on the mountain that first night, Alys couldn't guess.

He said, "It's not that late. I'll go to the village now and tell Gower that I need a wheel for a farm cart. Then, tomorrow, we'll both go to the village." He kept on talking though she had started to shake her head. "We'll place a bandage around your head and face so that nobody can get a proper look at you, and tell them your jaw is broken so you can't talk. I'll tell them you were injured when the wheel we bought from Gower broke. That way we've already started to chip away at his reputation *and* we'll say that we have nowhere to stay so Gower—feeling guilty—will have to put us up."

"Gower has never felt guilty about anything in his life," Alys said.

Selendrile shrugged, an indication, Alys supposed, that they'd worry about that when they came to it.

Alys once again tipped her face up to the night sky, annoyed that he could take all this so lightly. "The rest of it could work," she conceded.

When he didn't answer, she looked and saw that he'd never waited for her decision but had already started walking toward the road that led to Saint Toby's. Alys had to run to catch up. "Am I supposed to wait here, or what?" she demanded.

"Your decision," he said. "Though I'd have thought you'd be interested." He was making it sound as though she'd been wheedling not to go.

"That's not— Oh, never mind." With his longer stride, it took all her breath just to keep up without looking like a silly little puppy.

"Through the woods here." She pointed to where the road began the final curve before the village.

They stayed to the perimeter of Barlow's pasture so that the trees would hide them from anyone looking out a cottage window, for the moon was full and the night was bright. Then they cut across the corner of Wilfred's wheat field and so came upon Saint Toby's from behind.

"This is as far as I dare go," Alys whispered, crouching between rows of black currant bushes to make herself as small as possible. Selendrile stooped down also, resting his hands on her shoulders to look beyond her to where she pointed. "That's Gower's house, the one with the wagon wheel by the right-hand corner." Candlelight peeked out through the chinks by the window, though it must be getting close to bedtime. Next door, dark, was the house in which she'd been born and had lived all her fifteen years. Loneliness—the yearning for her father, for things to go back to the way they had been—swept over her. The house was close enough that—except for the fear of being seen—Alys could have run up and touched it in the time she would need to count to twenty.

Selendrile showed no inclination to move, so Alys said, "If you're going to be telling them that you're—we're—from one of the farms between here and Griswold, you'd better circle round to the front and approach openly."

He gave her a cold look, which could have meant that he'd thought of that already, or that she was being too loud, or any of a dozen other things. Without acknowledging her suggestion, without even standing, he moved back and disappeared between the bushes. Only he could have made such a move look graceful. If she had tried it, she'd have pitched forward onto her face.

Eventually Alys gave up trying to catch some telltale movement or rustle to betray his passage, and she sat down to wait, trusting that there was no reason for him to abandon her here. She propped her chin up on her hands and enjoyed the quiet of the night and the reassuringly familiar smell of good farming earth. She found her head beginning to nod when suddenly she caught sight of Selendrile approaching Gower's house, walking next to Gower's wife. Presumably Una had been out late visiting one of the households on the edge of the village when Selendrile had entered, and she must have offered to guide him to her husband's wheelwright's shop. But to Alys's dismay, she realized that while she could see well enough, she could hear absolutely nothing.

All unsuspecting, Una led the dragon-youth

to her door. She turned back to say something to him—Alys could see the flash of her smile in the moonlight—then she went in while Selendrile waited outside, never glancing in Alys's direction. Gower came out, and in an agony of frustration she watched the two of them talk. Gower kept shaking his head, but after a few moments, he entered his shop, and Selendrile sat down on the ground, leaning his back against the wall. That had to mean everything was going smoothly. Didn't it?

The back window opened, and daughter Etta dumped out a panful of water before securing the shutters again.

Una came out of the house carrying a steaming bowl, presumably left over from supper, and handed it to Selendrile.

Hmph! thought Alys, who had never gotten a free meal from Una despite the nearly dozen wheels she and her father had paid Gower to make.

Una went back inside and Selendrile tossed pieces of whatever it was Una had given him out into the street, where a suspicious, but apparently half-starving, dog gobbled them up, coming closer and closer, but warily.

You'll be HIS dinner next, Alys mentally warned the dog.

Una came back out, fanning herself with her hand as though the house was too warm, which Alys didn't believe for a moment. She'd seen the way the women of Griswold had looked at Selendrile, and even from this far away she could recognize that Una was giving him the same look. Maybe if Alys hadn't known what he was, he'd have had the same effect on her. But, she told herself, she wouldn't have been so obvious about it.

Gower came out of the shop, rolling a wheel before him. Selendrile returned the bowl to Una, no doubt with his usual charming smile. Alys could see him pay Gower, then lift the wheel up onto his back and start off down the road to the outskirts of the village.

Alys crawled along the row between the bushes, then cut off through the wood to meet him just beyond where the road curved.

Either he heard her coming despite the fact that she had deliberately moved as quietly as possible, or being a great hulking dragon had given him steady nerves, for he didn't flinch when she jumped out of the dark at him.

"I couldn't hear a thing," she told him. "What did he say?"

Selendrile positioned himself so that he was facing in the direction of Saint Toby's. He set the wheel down on its edge and looked at her over the top. "The shop closes at sundown and I have a lot of nerve interrupting a hardworking man's rest."

Alys glanced meaningfully at the wheel. "Obviously something changed his mind."

"The wife."

Alys snorted. "I can imagine."

Selendrile seemed to shift intent between the breath he took and the words. "Is there something specific you want to argue about, or are you just being generally unpleasant?"

Alys squirmed, but couldn't bring herself to apologize. "They didn't seem to suspect anything?"

"No."

"Una seemed in a rare talkative mood. What did she say?"

He looked beyond her as though to make sure no one from the village had followed. *"All* of it?" He sighed.

She tried to stifle a smile. "Just the important parts."

"There weren't any important parts."

This time Alys laughed, and Selendrile's attention shot back to her. "She was flirting with you," Alys explained, lest he think she was laughing at him. "She liked you."

Selendrile considered. His expression never changing from thoughtful innocence, he looked back toward Saint Toby's and said, "Maybe we can use that against her."

Chapter 11

ALYS FELT AS THOUGH she'd slept only moments when Selendrile shook her awake.

"What? What is it?" She was alert enough to know that she wasn't alert enough to cope if something had gone wrong. And something *had* gone wrong, or else why was Selendrile getting her up while it was still dark out?

Not that he seemed anxious or afraid, she realized as he pulled her up to a sitting position.

But then again, when had he ever?

Only slightly less groggy now, she asked, "Has something happened?"

By the way he paused to consider she could tell that nothing had, at least not in the sense she had meant.

"I broke the wheel," he said, "so that it would look as though the wood had been stressed then patched while Gower was making it."

"Yes," Alys said, for this was what they had decided earlier. "Fine. Good night."

He held on to her arm so that she couldn't lie back down. "It's almost dawn. And I brought these." He dropped a handful of rags onto her lap.

It took a moment for her to realize that what in the dim light looked like black patches was in fact blood. She flinched and his grip tightened. "I'm awake," she assured him. If she was going to claim to be injured, it only made sense to nave bandages that supported that claim. Still, she didn't ask where the blood had come from; and he didn't say. He just sat there looking at her.

The blood was still wet, though it had gone cold and sticky. Gingerly she draped one of the cloths over her head and around her chin, inwardly cringing at the touch of it against her cheek.

"Tighter," Selendrile advised. "You don't want it to sag, or they'll see that there's unbroken skin beneath." He took over, then sat back and evaluated his handiwork. He must have been satisfied, though she'd never have guessed from his face, because he picked up another cloth and began to wrap it around the knuckles of her right hand.

From between teeth which were clenched together from the tightness of his knot, Alys said, "I can't talk." Even she couldn't make out her words.

"What?"

Alys loosened the head cloth. "It's too tight. I can't talk."

Selendrile pulled it up tight again. "You don't need to be able to talk. You only need to be able to breathe. You *can* breathe, can't you?"

"Just barely." The words sounded garbled to her, and Alys doubted whether he'd understood. But apparently the fact that she was neither turning purple nor falling over onto her side and twitching satisfied him that she was getting enough air.

"If you talk," Selendrile said, "somebody might recognize your voice."

Alys sighed, knowing he was right.

"If you sigh around other people as much as

you sigh around me, somebody's bound to recognize that, too."

THEY REACHED the outskirts of Saint Toby's as the edge of the sky began to turn pink. Some of the villagers would be just getting up, Alys knew, though nobody was out and about yet.

Selendrile was dragging the damaged wheel and she was trying to remember to favor her right leg, which was supposed to be injured, in case anybody was watching. In front of Gower's home, she leaned against the wheel as though for support while Selendrile banged on the door, much louder than necessary to rouse just Gower's household. "Wheelwright!" he bellowed.

The door flung open, and there was Gower, holding a candle to see what the commotion was, looking as furious as a water-doused cat. At the sight of him, Alys's knees got weak and she was glad she had the wheel to support her after all.

"What's all this?" he demanded, looking straight at her.

She realized that she was breathing loudly, stopped, remembered that she was supposed to be hurt and that great wheezing breaths might be mistaken for exhaustion as well as panic, and resumed with a ragged intake of air.

"That wheel you sold us broke," Selendrile said, still overly loud. "My brother Jocko, here, has been injured."

Behind Gower, Etta and Una hovered in the doorway.

"My wheels don't break," Gower said.

Alys heard another villager's door open nearby and saw Gower's glance shift to the left.

"The wheel broke," Selendrile shouted. "Just look at my poor brother. This town was closer than our farm, so we came back here."

Yet another door opened a crack.

"Just"—Gower held his hands out, indicating there was no need for excitement in front of witnesses—"come inside."

Selendrile threw his arm around Alys as though she couldn't make it alone.

Gower shoved his daughter in the direction of the wheel. "Get that thing indoors," he commanded between clenched teeth.

Alys let Selendrile half drag, half carry her across the floor of the living area to the bed. Gower looked pretty sour about that, but Una lit a candle from the low-burning night-fire and brought it over.

Compassionate soul that she was, Etta made a disgusted face and put her back to them to get breakfast started.

With an expression that matched her daughter's, Una nodded toward Alys's head and said, "That probably needs a fresh bandage."

"No!" Alys mumble-cried. She couldn't be sure anybody could understand her, and she flinched away.

"No," Selendrile said quietly. "We had a terrible time getting the bleeding to stop. It's probably best to leave the wound alone."

For all that she'd gotten closer than her daughter had, Una looked relieved. "If you think that's best," she murmured.

Oh, for heaven's sake, Alys thought at the worshipful expression on the older woman's face.

"Never saw anything like this happen to one of my wheels before," Gower said, examining the wheel by the light of the fire.

"Well," Selendrile said charitably, "it can't be helped now. We're just lucky we weren't both killed when the cart tipped into the ditch."

"Oh my!" Una said breathlessly, never glancing away from Selendrile, not even to the wheel.

Slowly Selendrile looked up from Alys, flat on her back on Gower and Una's bed, and met Una's gaze. Even from this awkward position Alys could see his smile was dazzling. She groaned and burrowed deeper into the mattress.

"I'll make a new wheel for you," Gower said, heading for the workshop.

After he was gone, Selendrile said, "I should be going."

"What?" Alys cried, her voice muffled by the bandages.

"Must you leave?" Una asked.

Selendrile took Una's hand and held it gently between his own. With a look so sincere Alys wanted to choke, he said, "After the accident, Jocko and I just left the cart upturned in the ditch by the road, with the ox tethered so it could graze a bit without wandering off. I need to return it to the farm and make sure everything's all right there. Could you please watch over my brother until this evening?"

"Certainly," Una said, which Alys knew only meant that she wanted to see Selendrile again.

Between clenched teeth, Alys hissed, "Don't you dare leave me behind."

"What did he say?" Una was gazing at Selendrile in a dreamy sort of way.

"He said you're much too kind," Selendrile said, still looking deep into Una's eyes. "And you are. You're very kind."

Una modestly looked away. "I do what I can," she whispered.

Alys was tempted to demand, "Since when?" Instead she waited for Selendrile to once again lean over her.

"I'll be back as soon as I can, Jocko." He gently patted her shoulder.

With her supposed "good" hand, she grabbed a handful of shirt and, as distinctly as possible, whispered, "I'll get you for this."

"What did he say?" Una asked.

"I don't know." Selendrile turned and gazed at her sincerely. "After that knock on the head, he hasn't been making much sense lately. I think you just need to leave him alone all day—let him rest."

"Don't do this to me," Alys begged.

Without a word, he straightened, kissed Una's hand, and left.

Chapter 12

WHY WAS HE always doing this to her? Alys wondered: helping her, guiding her, tricking her into trusting him—*liking* him even—though all her instincts warned against either, and then repeatedly tossing her out on her own, forcing her to plot and make decisions and confront her enemies all by herself?

She burrowed deeper into the bedding and lowered her eyelids so that they were open only the slightest crack, pretending sleep. Una still stood by the door, shifting her gaze from her hand to the path Selendrile had taken. Wherever she looked, she wore an expression that reminded Alys of the large moist eyes of particularly loyal and brainless cows. Alys thought of the dog Selendrile had been feeding last night.

At least *it* had had the sense to be afraid. And at least *it* was getting food out of the relationship.

As though suddenly aware of what she was doing, Una cast quick looks at Alys and beyond, presumably to Etta, who was noisily setting out the breakfast meal. Apparently satisfied that no one had been watching, Una moved out of Alys's range of vision to help Etta.

"Here," she heard Una say, "go put this by him."

"But he's disgusting," Etta protested. "He's all bloody and"—Alys could just picture the wince—"dirty."

"Hush your mouth and do as I say."

Etta sneered, "*You* do it then if you're so taken by him and his brother." Then, "All right, *all right, ALL RIGHT,*" she squealed in a tone that made Alys suspect Una was twisting her ear.

Through the quivery slits between her eyelashes, Alys watched Etta gingerly approach. She stopped while still at least six feet away, then put the steaming wooden bowl on the floor and eased it somewhat closer to the bed with her foot, slopping grayish gruel over the edges.

Alys grumbled and snorted sleepily and Etta scampered away.

Eating in front of anyone was too dangerous: She'd have to loosen the bandages and they would easily see that she wasn't nearly so badly hurt as they'd been led to believe. With nothing better to do while she pretended to sleep, Alys actually did fall asleep.

When she awoke, she was alone. She could hear Gower in his shop next door hammering, a sound she had heard all her life. There was no sign of Etta, but Alys could hear Una talking outside, complaining to someone about the heat this summer. As far back as Alys could remember, Una had always complained; the weather was always too hot for her—or too cold, or too dry, or too windy, or too changeable. Possibly because she was just waking up, a wisp of laughter floated into Alys's memory. She thought of her friend Risa, who had died after stepping on a rusty nail the summer she was eight. Risa had been able to do a wonderful imitation of Una: "It's too...it's too...it's too *perfect*, for my taste," Risa would say, tossing her hair.

From the direction of the stream where the village women washed their clothes, Alys could very faintly hear singing, a sweet high voice that could only be Aldercy, who—until she'd put aside girlish interests and girlhood friends to get married—had been Alys's friend.

Without warning, Alys's eyes were suddenly full of tears. *Things weren't horrible in Saint Toby's before,* she thought. *I want to go back, I want to go back.* She wiped her nose roughly to bring herself to her senses. Her father was dead; there was no going back. Instead, she got up and fetched the bowl Etta had set out for her. She probably shouldn't have had the strength to do it on her own, but not eating could result in real weakness. She loosened the bandages. Though the meal was cold and congealed into thick lumps, she ate it in quick mouthfuls lest someone enter and find her at it.

Finished, she tied up the bandages again, lay back down, and hoped that whatever Selendrile was up to, he'd be quick at it.

Lying on the straw mattress, waiting, she thought about the years during which she had grown up in Saint Toby's, playing with her friends: the hoop games they had made with old wheels, the games of jackstraws, and the straw dolls they used to make. And with that she suddenly knew how to trap Etta. Everybody knew that village girls weren't the only ones to make straw dolls. Witches did, too, except theirs were made in the image of a particular person. Then, when the right spell was spoken, whatever the witch did to the doll would happen to the real person. Alys got up again.

Working hurriedly, she pulled a handful of straw from the mattress and fashioned a doll, folding the straw in half and tying off the head, then braiding arms and legs. She found a rag, which she wrapped around the figure for clothes, then pulled a tin button off Etta's feast-day dress. For a long moment she held the button, knowing that it was her father's hands which had poured the metal, then shaped it. She was torn between the desire to keep it and the knowledge that putting tin on the doll would make people think it had been imaged after the tinsmith's daughter.

"I'll make them sorry, Papa," she whispered, though her father had never been the kind of man to seek revenge on anyone.

Alys fastened the button to the doll, then got

a stick from the woodpile by the hearth and fastened the doll to the stick. Hopefully, when the villagers saw this, they would think that Etta had compelled them to condemn her, to leave her tied up on the mountain for the dragon.

Seeing the completed doll in her own image, Alys felt strangely unsettled. Although she knew she had no witch's power, she whispered out loud—three times, since that was the way with spells—"Not Alys. Not Alys. Not Alys," just to be safe. Then she hid the doll under Etta's mattress and lay down. She'd worry later about how to bring it to everyone's attention.

Eventually she fell asleep again.

Eventually she woke up again.

Slowly the day passed, and when Selendrile finally returned, it was already late evening.

"Welcome back." Una scrambled up from the table where she and her family were having supper to greet him. She wiped her hands on her apron. "I hope you found everything in order back at your farm." Gower glanced up to scowl at Selendrile; Etta never stopped shoveling food into her mouth, as though afraid somebody'd eat her portion if she let her attention wander.

Alys groaned and stretched as though Una's greeting had awakened her.

"Everything's as it should be." Selendrile took Una's hand in his and smiled into her eyes.

Una blushed and acted surprised, as though she hadn't wiped her hands hoping for just this.

"And how's my little brother?" Selendrile knelt beside Alys's bed.

"I hate you," she murmured into his ear. "Without you, the plan's going all wrong."

"What?" Una asked.

"He said better, thank you, but he feels weak from lying down for so long." Selendrile grabbed her by her unbandaged arm and pulled her to her feet. "There," he said chipperly, "how's that?"

She glared at him. "Now I'm supposed to be able to walk?" she asked.

"You want to go for a walk?" Selendrile said. "I'm not sure that's for the best."

She started to sit back down, but he held her where she was.

"Well, if you insist. But slowly." He smiled and nodded to the others and led her toward the door.

"What are you doing?" she demanded.

"You're doing fine," he assured her.

She sighed and didn't try to get any more out of him until they were outside. They walked very slowly, with her leaning heavily on his shoulder because many of the villagers were out, pointing at her and saying, "There's the poor boy hurt when Gower's wheel failed."

Alys loosened the bandage slightly. "We're going too far," she warned. "If we talk quietly, nobody'll hear us. If I'm supposed to be half dying, I shouldn't be able to walk this far."

Smiling and nodding at someone across the way, Selendrile said, "We can always say you overextended yourself. I'll carry you back."

"You will not," Alys told him.

He smiled but didn't answer till they were beyond the last cottage. "So," he said, "what have you done all day?"

"What have *I* done?" Alys pulled away from his encircling arm and sat on a log by the side of the road. "What have *you* done?"

Selendrile shrugged. "Nothing. I've just been waiting for evening."

"*What?*"

"Nothing. I've just been w—"

"Why?"

He paused to look at her before answering. "Evenings are more romantic."

"What?"

He sighed, sounding annoyed, either at her limited range of questions or at her tone. "Humans find moonlight romantic, right? You want me to flirt with Una, right? Why are you getting all upset when I'm doing exactly what you told me to do?"

"I never told you..." Alys rested her head in her hand, exasperated at the loss of a whole day.

"Besides," he added, "we don't want to arouse suspicion by working too fast."

"All right," she said.

"Besides—"

"All right." She pulled the bandage entirely away from her face so she could speak properly. "I've been thinking more about the plan. We want everyone to believe Gower is making bad wheels, so we started with the wheel he made for us. Can you damage some of the ones he's made for other people?"

"Me?" Selendrile asked.

"Maybe by turning into a mouse and gnawing at a spoke here and there? Just a little bit, as though Gower gouged the wood while working it and didn't bother starting over?"

Slowly he nodded.

"As for Una...Eventually what we want is for her to leave Gower for you." Selendrile didn't react. "Slowly, over the next two or three days, we want her to fall in love with you, make a fool of herself in front of the other villagers."

His voice giving away nothing of what he thought, he asked, "Somebody falling in love with me would look foolish to the villagers?"

"No." Even in the moonlight she found herself distracted by the purple of his eyes. She looked away, suddenly confused. "No. I just mean...a married woman, with a daughter your age..." He arched his eyebrows. "...the age you seem..." She forced herself to meet his eyes again. "It'll look foolish for Una."

"Ah," he said.

"So that when you ask her to run away with you, to meet you in Griswold, and then you never show up there, she'll be too ashamed to come back to Saint Toby's because everyone will know where she went and why."

Once more Selendrile nodded.

"As for Etta, I made a straw image of myself

and hid it in her things. Now all we have to do is get people to look—just like we did with Atherton. I thought maybe you can turn yourself into a crow and follow her around—witches always have crows."

Selendrile didn't look convinced about that one.

"And every time she has an argument with one of her friends—she's always having arguments—we can do something to the friend."

"Something like what?"

"I don't know. It didn't take much for them to believe *I* was a witch."

"Cause them to fall down stairs?" Selendrile suggested. He looked interested again. Maybe too interested. "Have their geese or chickens disappear? Perhaps burn down a few houses? Something like that?"

Alys squirmed. "Something like that."

"I see."

"We'll discuss it beforehand, for each person."

"Certainly," he said with a smoothness she didn't like at all.

"Maybe," Alys started, "you—"

Selendrile lunged at her.

Alys didn't have time to gasp before he had one hand on her shoulder and the other ... Suddenly she realized what he was doing: shoving the bloodied bandage up by her jaw. In another moment, even as she scrambled to tighten the cloth back around her head, she heard the sound of approaching footsteps and the jangle of metal.

The bandage wasn't as secure as it should have been when a man came around the corner from the direction of Saint Toby's. Alys tried to disguise her sigh of relief. The man was a stranger—obviously a wandering peddler: He had pots and crocks and assorted other merchandise lashed to his back and chest and belt.

"Hello, my friends, hello," he said in a loud, squeaky voice that hurt Alys's ears. He flashed a smile that showed good strong teeth despite the shabbiness of his clothes and the fact that he was dirty and had a patch over his right eye. He pointed at Alys. "You must be that young lad I heard tell about what got hurt in that farm-cart accident."

Alys nodded, holding the bandage with her hand, unsure whether it might come loose.

"I just been in town a few hours, but already I heard all about it from everybody. Everybody's talking. Terrible thing, terrible thing. I told that woman, the wheelwright's wife, I got just the thing for you, but she wouldn't let me in the house, more's the shame, but now, just as I'm leaving, here you are."

Here I am, Alys thought. Trust it to her luck that the man wasn't going to spend the night at Saint Toby's like any normal peddler but would set out again this late.

The man was disentangling himself from the various bags and harness that held his wares. "I have," he repeated, "just the thing."

"That's very kind of you," Alys mumbled into the bandage, "but really we don't have any money anyway—"

"No, no, I'll have it in a moment." With his one pale brown eye, he looked up from pawing through the contents of his bags. "Silver it is," he said. "Where am I going to sell silver in villages like this? But it has healing properties. That'll make it worth more, you say?" He waggled a dirty finger at her. "But it's not for sale. It's for giving. An old woman without enough money to put beans in her soup gave it to me when I caught the flux last winter. She said, 'I'll give you this-here bracelet, like someone gave it to me, and someone before that gave it to her, and when you're through with it you must give it away, too.'" He went back to looking through his bag. "That's where the magic is, don't you know, in the giving it away."

Alys glanced at Selendrile, who shrugged.

"Here it is." The peddler pulled something out of his bag with a flourish, but Alys couldn't get a good look at it. "Hmmm," he said, "it should probably go on your injured arm. You"—he indicated Selendrile—"hold the lad's arm out straight, and I'll put it on."

It seemed the fastest way to get rid of him. Alys gave a nod to Selendrile, who helped support her arm as though it were sore.

After seeing all the real silver that she had in the past couple of days, Alys caught one glimpse of the peddler's so-called silver bracelet and knew it was too dull, too heavy to be real. If he thought he was going to talk her into—

But before Alys could finish the thought, the peddler shoved her so that she fell off the log, causing the bandage to drop away from her face entirely.

She didn't have time to worry about that, for in the same instant he snapped the bracelet around Selendrile's arm and Selendrile cried out as though the metal burned. But before he could seize the bracelet off, the peddler swung one of his huge pots and cracked Selendrile across the side of the head with it.

Selendrile collapsed to the ground just as Alys sprang to her feet and leaped at the man. He hit her in the stomach with his elbow; then, when she doubled over, he ran into her so that they fell to the ground, him on top of her.

She tried to rake her fingers across his face, but he turned so that she only ripped off the eye patch before he had both her hands pinned to the ground on either side of her head. Two perfectly whole and healthy pale brown eyes looked down at her, and then the peddler smiled.

"Atherton!" she gasped.

Chapter 13

ATHERTON FLIPPED her facedown into the dirt and dragged her hands behind her back.

"Selendrile!" she cried as the Inquisitor twisted rope around her wrists. "Selendrile!"

But when Atherton finally got up, removing his knee from the small of her back, she was able to see the dragon-youth still sprawled motionless on the ground.

Backing away from her, his eyes shifting warily from her to Selendrile, Atherton approached his dropped peddler's pack. *Be pretending,* she thought at Selendrile as Atherton fished out another metal band, this one attached to a short length of chain. *Grab him as soon as he comes near.*

But Selendrile made no move as Atherton used the bands and chain to shackle his arms behind his back. Only when the dragon-youth was safely bound did Atherton nudge him onto his side. "Get up," he commanded. When a rough shake got no reaction, he slapped him hard enough that Alys winced.

Selendrile groaned and stirred, and Atherton sidled away from him.

"Coward," Alys jeered.

Atherton jerked her to her feet and shoved her at Selendrile. "Get him up and get him to cooperate, or I'll kill him here and now." Atherton pulled a short, broad dagger from his belt. He held it under her chin so that the point pressed against her skin just short of cutting. "Don't assume that as a man of the Church I'll stay my hand from doing it. I know what that creature is—spawn of Satan, evil incarnate. And your association with ... *it* ... proves that you are the same."

Alys didn't pause to try to reason out how Atherton could know that Selendrile wasn't what he appeared. "You're more evil—"

He slapped her, hard. All her fifteen years, no one had ever hit her before. Even during the trial, even with all the roughness edged with the threat of death, no one had struck her.

Be careful, she warned herself. Atherton seemed dangerously close to mindless violence. At least for the moment he apparently wanted them alive, and she had to take care not to change that.

With a deep breath she knelt beside Selendrile. What was she supposed to do, with her hands tied behind her back? She nudged him with her knee. "Selendrile. We're in trouble. Get up."

Again he groaned, then he caught his breath as though in pain. Still, she couldn't see any blood where Atherton had hit him. Maybe he wasn't too badly hurt after all.

"Selendrile," she repeated.

He opened his eyes slowly, gingerly.

"It's Atherton," she told him. "Atherton's here."

Selendrile winced, then kept his eyes closed.

Alys heard Atherton take a step closer. "Selendrile, get up," she begged, knowing that Atherton would consider driving the dagger into his heart as an act of faith in God. "I can't help you. He's tied my hands, too."

Selendrile forced himself to sit up, though he swayed dizzily.

Alys followed his gaze and saw Atherton pouring liquid from a vial into his hand. *Now what?* She jerked as he spattered it onto their upturned faces, but it didn't hurt. *Water,* she realized; and, a moment later, *Holy water.* If he was expecting that they would go up in flames or that their skin would peel off, he must have been disappointed. But no, he seemed satisfied that they'd both flinched, as though this proved more than that they'd been startled.

Do something, she mentally urged Selendrile, wondering why he was so sluggish, why he didn't transform into something big and powerful and fierce.

Atherton put the vial back into his pack and once again waved the dagger. "Up, both of you."

"Can't you see he's hurt?" Alys said. "With that blow to his head, he won't be able to make it back to Saint Toby's without help."

Atherton snorted. *"Blow to his head,"* he sneered. "It's the iron shackles. Iron to bind the fey. He won't be able to take on other shapes until I remove the iron."

Alys looked to Selendrile to see if this was true. His teeth were clenched with what might have been pain or loathing or both, and his breathing was still ragged. She saw that his face was pale and damp with sweat. The last of her hope seeped out of her. "You should have told me," she said softly.

He looked at her but said nothing.

Atherton said, "Now *get up*."

Alys scrambled to her feet. Selendrile followed more slowly, still looking unsteady.

"And as for Saint Toby's," Atherton said, "I don't care one whit about that foul little place or anybody in it. We're going back to Griswold, where you'll publicly admit what you did and why. You'll bare your black little soul for everyone, and then they'll know how they wronged me. Then they'll see what you are. Then you'll know what it's like..." He'd grabbed the collar of her shirt and raised his hand, the one with the knife in it.

He'd forgotten he held it, she was sure, and he was only intending to hit her, but instead he was going to kill her and her arms were tied behind her and there was nothing she could do to protect herself. She shrank away as far as she could, which wasn't far enough, from the knife, from the crazed look in his eyes.

Atherton didn't strike. He only repeated, "Then you'll know what it's like."

She didn't say that she already knew what it was like. "I'll tell them nothing," she said. "If you're going to kill us anyway, why should I cooperate?"

"For a fast death by fire," he told her, "rather than by knives, inch by inch for days and days. And days." He was breathing as unsteadily as Selendrile. "For this favor, you will tell them everything, and you will buy back my soul."

For a moment she thought he meant that her admission of guilt would buy back his honor, his reputation.

But then in one giddy realization she knew what he really meant.

And how he'd escaped the angry mob in Griswold.

And where he'd learned what Selendrile really was, and how iron would bind him.

"The witch in the glen," she whispered. "You sold your soul to her to get revenge on me."

"And when we get back there, you'll tell her that you'll take my place." Atherton flung her away from him so that, without her arms to balance herself, she fell down on one knee on the road. "Move," he snarled, indicating the direction toward Griswold.

WITH ATHERTON WALKING behind them, Alys didn't even try to squirm loose of the rope. What good would it do when, in the moonlight, he could see every move?

Beside her, Selendrile was shivering, and several times Atherton prodded him to get him moving faster. Once he stumbled and fell, and Atherton dragged him back to his feet by the hair. The second time, Atherton began screaming at him and strode forward so purposefully, with his dagger ready, that Alys threw herself to her knees behind him to protect his back. "Get up," she begged.

Selendrile leaned against her, and she thought he was too weak to go any farther. But possibly he drew strength from her, for he managed to stagger to his feet before Atherton could separate them.

The Inquisitor pulled her up by her shirt.

"Harm him and I'll never admit to anything," she warned.

Atherton just smiled at her, as coldly as Selendrile had ever done.

She thought he meant to walk all the way to Griswold that very night, but he stopped when they reached the hilltop where Alys had been condemned to die.

"We'll rest here," Atherton smirked, standing before the pole to which she'd been tied. "For old times' sake." He tucked his dagger into its sheath on his belt. Then, before she knew what was happening, he hooked his leg around hers and sent her sprawling.

From the ground, she saw him yank up on the chain that connected Selendrile's shackles, twisting the iron into his flesh. Selendrile gasped in pain and his knees buckled. Atherton yanked again, forcing him to fall into a sitting position, his back almost against the pole.

And suddenly, as Atherton reached into the leather pouch on his belt, Alys knew what he was doing.

He was counting on the dragon-youth being too overwhelmed with pain to resist being secured to the pole, but he'd made a mistake knocking her down where she stood rather than commanding her to move away and to keep her back to them. As soon as he unlocked the left shackle, Alys leaped to her feet and ran at him, head lowered like a goat.

With his own head bent down, concentrating on watching Selendrile, Atherton didn't see her till the last moment. He had time to turn to take the blow on his upper arm rather than his chest, but all three of them went sprawling in a tangle of arms and legs.

Having the use of both arms, Atherton recovered first and pulled himself to his knees. But rather than lashing out at either of them or going for his dagger, he did the worst possible thing: He hurled the key into the surrounding forest.

In another moment Selendrile whipped the loose chain around the Inquisitor's neck. The iron must have cut deeply into his own wrist and hands, but he tightened the chain and kept it up and kept it up until Alys, lying on her stomach with her face lifted up from the grass, realized that he wasn't going to let go. Certainly she had seen people die before, even her own father not four days since. But she'd never seen someone being killed before. "Selendrile," she said as Atherton's fingers scrabbled, weaker and weaker now, at the chain. "Selendrile!"

He looked up at her. His purple eyes met hers. Held hers. And still he didn't release the chain.

What had she done? As foul as Atherton was, she couldn't just stand by and watch him die. "Stop it," she told Selendrile. She scrambled to her feet, but by then Atherton's eyes rolled upward and he went limp against Selendrile.

Slumped over like that, he looked too much like her own father in Gower's storeroom.

"Stop!"

Still Selendrile didn't let go and didn't let go, and when he did, finally, it was only after giving the chain a final vicious tug, and—even if the Inquisitor hadn't been dead before—Alys heard his neck snap.

Now, slowly, Selendrile stood, too. The eyes that had looked so cool, so emotionless during the killing, now smoldered. "Stop?" he said. "Now? Isn't this what you wanted? Isn't this what you asked me to do?" He grabbed her by the shoulders and shook her.

"Yes," she said softly, and wondered: *What have I done?* Fly over the village, she'd told him, breathing fire and roasting them all, down to the last baby. She swallowed. "It's exactly what I asked you to do."

He seemed to suddenly feel the drag of the chain on his wrist and he let her go. Moving slowly, he got the dagger from Atherton's belt, holding it carefully by the wooden handle. Just how angry was he? Alys asked herself, warily watching his approach, afraid of him once more. She had talked herself into believing that— deep down—he was like her, thought like her, felt like her. She held her breath. But he only turned her around and cut through the rope that held her. Then, letting the dagger drop, he staggered several steps away before sitting down heavily on the ground. Too hurt to move? But he was running his left hand through the grass.

A moment later she realized he was searching for the key. Iron to bind the fey, Atherton had said. His death hadn't changed that. "You're not looking far enough." She carefully avoided looking at the body. "He threw it into the trees."

He glanced up at her but said nothing.

Alys went to the line of trees, where the

branches blocked the moonlight, and she had to get down on her hands and knees to feel the ground. She found little stones, and leaves and twigs from autumns gone by, but no key.

Perhaps it had landed farther away than she'd thought. She crawled farther, and farther, past the point where it could conceivably have reached, to the left and right of where she'd seen it fly, and still no sign of it.

She looked up through the trees back into the clearing. Annoyed, she saw that Selendrile was sitting exactly where she had left him, which just went to show that the key couldn't be *that* important to him. "Well," she said, wiping her gritty hands on her breeches, "we'll wait until morning, see if it's any easier to find in the daylight. If not, we'll have to think of some story to tell the blacksmith in Griswold, and have him cut the shackles off."

By this time, she'd made it back to him, and he looked up at her with that same calm expression he'd had while killing Atherton. "By morning I'll be dead."

She would have accused him of exaggerating, except that his level tone was like ice down her back. *Iron to bind the fey.* She had seen that it was poisoning him and she had refused to acknowledge it. She knelt down in front of him. His wrists were bruised and raw, though she could see from his still-bound right wrist that the iron band was loose enough that it could twist around freely. Not loose enough to slip over his hand though. The mechanism could tighten by pushing, but needed a key to loosen. "Maybe if we ripped your shirt—or Atherton's—and wrapped the fabric around the iron to protect the skin—we'll start out for Griswold immediately—or Saint Toby's, that's closer, although I don't know what we'll tell them—or—"

"Alys," he said, and it was the first time he'd ever called her by her real name. It made her stop, wait, while he closed his eyes and took a deep breath. "I can't change back into a dragon while I'm bound by the iron."

"Yes," she said.

"And I have to be a dragon come dawn or I'll die."

"Why?"

"*Why?*" He sighed, sounding more tired than exasperated. "Why can't you soar on the wind? Why can't you breathe underwater? Why can't you shed your skin and turn into a butterfly?"

She didn't understand. But she believed.

"All right," she said. He couldn't die now. Not after all this. "The night's not even half gone. We'll walk back to Saint Toby's..." She drifted off because he was shaking his head, and in fact she could see it as well as he: He'd scarcely made it here; there was no way he could walk all the way back to Saint Toby's. "All right," she said again. "*I'll* go. I'll *run* back to Saint Toby's. I'll get one of my father's metal-cutting tools and run back here with it. I'll—"

"There's not enough time," Selendrile interrupted her.

He might have been right. Or not. She couldn't be sure. "Well, what *should* we do?" she demanded.

Selendrile shook his head. "I don't know." His voice was soft, hopeless. "I've run out of plans."

"I'll go to Saint Toby's, then. You can keep looking for the key." He started to protest and she talked over his objections. "You *might* find it. Maybe. It's better than doing nothing."

There was just a flicker of fear in the set of his mouth, and then he lowered his eyes, accepting her judgment. And that was when she knew that he didn't believe that she'd be back, or at least not in time; but he was too proud to ask her not to let him die alone.

"I'm not going to abandon you," she promised him. "I'll be back, and I'll be back in time." She threw her arms around him and gave him a quick kiss, too quick for him to be able to respond, even if dragons knew how. But he caught her hand in his, which was, she knew, as close as he'd come to asking her to stay. She wanted to linger, to reassure him, but knew she might need the time that it would take. She pulled away. "I'm sure I can be back," she told him.

But she wasn't sure.

Chapter 14

ALYS RAN WHERE the path permitted, and fretted when tree roots or knife-pricks of exhaustion forced her to slow. Feebleminded, that's what she was. Selendrile had admitted from the first that he was a liar, and if she'd stopped to think about it she'd have known that the greater part of lying was not telling everything. How could she have assumed that he'd freely share his limitations? She'd had to guess that he couldn't speak except when he was in human form; how then could it have escaped her notice that he was always somewhere else during daylight hours?

It wasn't fair if he died because she hadn't been paying attention.

Especially now, having Atherton's death on his soul.

If he *had* a soul.

"He didn't mean it," she said out loud, meaning the words for God. "He doesn't think the way people do, and anyway he did it for me."

Speaking took the last of her breath and she had to stop, hands braced against her knees, panting. She thought, for the first time, about what it meant to be without a soul. Not petty and cruel, which Atherton had always been, but actually lacking a soul. Certainly Atherton's dead body didn't look significantly different from her father's. Would it? *Could* a soul be bougnt or traded, like woven baskets or salted fish? The more Alys thought about it, the less she believed so. And yet ... and yet, she thought, she herself had come dangerously close—not to selling her soul, but to giving it away, to throwing it away—in her search for revenge. And she hadn't needed the help of the witch in the glen to do it.

"He's sorry," Alys gasped to God. "I know he is. *I'm* sorry. Please don't let him die."

Surely the fact that Atherton had been planning to let Selendrile die should count for something.

As soon as she caught her breath, she once again began running.

When she—finally—approached the last curve before Saint Toby's, she tried to gauge how long she'd been and how much time was left. But she couldn't be sure. There was no sign of the sky becoming lighter in the east, which would have meant there definitely wasn't time to get back. But this way it was an agonizing case of maybe she could, and maybe she couldn't.

The village was still, no candles burning, the houses black blocks beneath the moon. She slowed to a walk, which was quieter than running, and approached the door to the tin shop. Saint Toby's was too small for locks, but there was a latch on the door to keep it from blowing open. Alys lifted the wooden beam out of the slot and gently lowered it.

The door creaked as she pushed, and she paused, thinking her heart would stop from the fear of getting caught. She fought her instinct to bolt, to hide in the surrounding darkness of the trees. Surely the noise seemed louder to her than it really was. From all around her in the village she heard nothing out of the ordinary, nothing to suggest anyone had heard or was watching. She stepped into the shop and slowly, slowly leaned against the door, pushing it shut as the hinges again screeched.

She blinked, waiting for her eyes to adjust to the darkness.

They didn't.

There was a window on the far wall, she knew even though she couldn't see it. Even the little bit of light she'd get from opening the shutters would be enough for her to find her way around this shop, which had always been a part of her life. But it was different, it didn't feel the same knowing that her father would never be back. She'd find a tool with which to cut Selendrile's one remaining shackle and be out of here in the time it would take to say two *Pater Nosters*.

Carefully she slid her feet across the packed-dirt floor so that she wouldn't trip over anything that wasn't where she remembered. On the third slide, her foot struck something—a table leg?—which had no business being there. Instinctively she straightened her arms in front of her. But it wasn't a table leg; it was a wagon wheel resting upright. And as her left hand caught it in time to keep it from tipping over, her right hand upset a metal bucket that was hanging from a nail on the wall. She lunged for the falling bucket, caught it at the same instant the wheel fell over onto her foot, dropped the bucket—which clattered against the wall, the wheel, and the floor, all the while emptying itself of what had to be half the world's supply of nails—then she lost her balance and fell down, knocking over two boards and a broom.

Alys sat on the floor where she'd landed, holding her breath, waiting for someone to come in and kill her.

Nothing, nobody stirred.

A wheel. It was a wheel she'd tumbled over. Gower hadn't wasted a moment taking over her father's shop.

Once she stopped shaking, she got to her hands and knees very slowly and crawled to the door. She opened it a crack and peeked out into the street. Much good stealth would do now that the door had once again shrieked on its hinges, announcing her intent.

As far as she could see, nobody was coming.

Alys took a deep breath and stood.

The open door illuminated the shop some-what. And anyway, she couldn't very well flee, knowing that that would condemn Selendrile to death. Unless, of course, he'd somehow found the key—which she didn't believe for a mo-ment. She picked her way across the rubble she'd made on the floor and headed toward the cabinet where her father had kept the smaller of his tools. As she'd expected, they were gone, re-placed by the wheelwright's equipment. Why hadn't she noticed the smell of fresh-cut wood and shavings before? Still, there had to be something here she could use. Chisels, awls, a mallet.

She had just put her hand out to sort through the tools when someone seized her elbow and spun her around, flinging her hard against the wall.

"I thought I'd—" Gower's eyes narrowed in recognition. "You," he said with such feeling that Alys knew he saw beyond the boy's cloth-ing and filthy face of the "injured boy" who'd been his houseguest. "Ahh," he continued, "now I understand what's been going on."

This was no time to be meek. "Do you think people will believe you?" Alys demanded. "Wheels that fall apart, wife ready to run off with the first handsome young stranger, daughter dabbling in magic—have they started to talk yet?"

By the way he shook her, she knew they had. "You'll come with me, girl, and everyone'll know you're behind it all soon's they see you. All they got to do is catch one look at you in them boy's clothes. Soon's they start wondering how you got away from that dragon, they won't care about any wheels." He started to pull her toward the door.

Alys dug her heels into the floor. "Selendrile rescued me from the dragon." That much was certainly true. "And as for coming back here, that proves my innocence. If I was really a witch, I'd have cast a spell and been done with all of you. There'd have been no reason to come back. Etta's the witch."

Gower paused while he tried to reason it out. Then, "No," he said, tugging again, "they'll know it was you."

"I'll deny it. And there'll always be that

doubt. Any time anything goes wrong, they'll wonder." She caught hold of the doorway before he could drag her outside. "But it doesn't have to be that way."

He tugged and it felt as though her fingers were going to fall off.

"Gower, it doesn't have to be that way."

He finally hesitated. "What are you saying?"

"I'll admit to everything. I'll clear your name, restore your family's reputation."

"In exchange for what?"

"For you letting me go."

"What?" Once again he started yanking at her, even while she said, "I'll come back, on my honor I will."

"The honor of a witch?" he scoffed. "A witch who's given herself to the devil—"

Alys held on to the door and looked him in the eyes. "You know I'm not a witch," she said.

It was Gower who looked away.

"Come with me, if you're afraid I'll run off," she said, which was casting away any last chance at freedom. "We'll be back here in time for the noonday meal. And I'll remove all trace of doubt from your name. I'll even confess to being a witch, so that no one will ever be able to claim you had an innocent girl put to death. No one will ever come after Etta."

Gower repeated: "In exchange for what?"

"Selendrile's in trouble."

"Is he now?" Gower interrupted with a snort.

"Inquisitor Atherton took us to the same place where you left me for the dragon. He shackled him to the same stake." The rest, she thought, it was better if he didn't know.

"I see," Gower said. "I go with you out to the wilds between here and Griswold, rescue your friend who promptly thanks me by slitting my throat—"

"He won't. I'll tell him not to, that you and I have come to an agreement."

He was considering it, she could tell.

"If we don't get there by dawn, the deal is off," she warned. "You saw how easily the villagers turned on me—do you think it'll be any different for Etta?"

"Let me think."

"If we don't get there by dawn, the deal is off," she screamed at him. Thinking was the last thing she wanted him to do. How much time had he wasted already?

"You swear I'll come to no harm?"

"Yes!"

"You swear you'll tell them you're a witch and that you arranged—"

"Yes!"

He was determined to get it all out. "—that you arranged for the wheel to break, that you bewitched my wife and daughter?"

"Yes, yes!" Then, as he paused to make sure he hadn't left anything out, she said, "Now, Gower."

Slowly he nodded.

"They're iron shackles," she said, lest she give him time to change his mind. "What do you have that'll cut through them?"

"Is it high-grade iron?"

"I don't know," she cried. "Gower!"

"All right, all right." He fetched a metal file. "This should work."

"Fine. Let's go."

Gower tucked the file into his belt. "Soon's I tell Una, so she doesn't worry."

From what she'd seen, Alys didn't think Una would worry if she found her husband sprouting tree branches from his head, but this didn't seem the time to say so. She trailed after

Gower, praying he wouldn't give enough details that either he or Una would start to question his decision.

Apparently Una wasn't so worried that she had stayed awake. Watching from the doorway, Alys saw Gower nudge his wife. "I'll be back," he told her.

Una grunted, which might have meant, "All right," or "Leave me alone." In any case, Gower lit a torch from the night-fire and came right back out.

"Hurry up," Alys told him.

"Listen, if he's shackled, he's not going anywhere. We'll be there soon enough."

"We'll be there before dawn," Alys repeated.

Gower scowled, but began walking faster.

Chapter 15

THE SKY WAS getting lighter, Alys was certain. If they'd been back at Saint Toby's with its open view, she'd have seen pink and orange streaks creeping up from the horizon. Instead, she and Gower were surrounded by trees that were steadily becoming more distinct, and by glimpses of sky shading from black to gray. Before, while she'd been hurrying in the opposite direction, she'd played a mental game with herself, saying, "If I get to here before the sky starts to lighten, then I'll be able to reach Selendrile in time." She'd said it just beyond the edge of the clearing where she'd left him, giving herself ample time to struggle with getting the shackle off. She'd said it further and further out, having to assume the shackle would be easier and easier to remove. She'd said it the last time at a point where she'd have had to run faster than she'd ever run before and where the shackle would have to drop off at a touch.

But now she and Gower had not even reached that point yet, and as the sky paled she was faced with the certain knowledge that there was no way she could reach Selendrile in time.

"It's not fair!" she cried out, and Gower gave her a wary look. It wasn't fair if Selendrile died from helping her. "Hurry up!" she told Gower, though they were both panting already.

He stopped to shift the torch to his left hand.

"Hurry up!" she came back to tell him.

He caught hold of her arm. "Why the rush?" he demanded.

"Not now." She tried to shake him loose, but he'd been put off and ordered around long enough.

"Why the rush?"

"Let go of me!" She was being foolish, she knew it but couldn't help herself. Gower wasn't preventing her from getting to Selendrile in time—there *was* no time. And yet to stand here bickering with the wheelwright while Selendrile

died alone . . . as he had been afraid he would. . . .
As—

The realization struck her that he would have no way of knowing that she had even tried. For all he knew, she may have never intended to return. *Could* he think that of her? Yes, he could, for, really, that would have been the most sensible thing for her to do, it would have been a *dragon* thing to do, and she remembered the expression on his face. "Selendrile!" she shouted with all her might, still trying to pull free of Gower. "I'm coming!" The important thing was not to convince him that she'd reach him in time; the important thing was to let him know she was coming back for him.

But it was hopeless in either case. Her voice could no more travel those extra miles to the clearing than she could.

"Girl . . ." Gower shook her.

With her free hand, she slapped him.

Looking more startled than hurt, he loosened his grip just as she once more tugged, and she tumbled into the weeds by the side of the path. This was the fourth time this night that she'd found herself sprawled on the ground.

There wasn't time to scramble to her feet and elude Gower, who was even now coming toward her; the best she could do was to once again yell Selendrile's name from where she lay, flat on her back.

Just as she opened her mouth, she heard, faintly: "Alys."

It was impossible. There was no way Selendrile could yell loud enough from the clearing that she could hear him here. Only her imagination told her otherwise.

But Gower had paused midstride, his head cocked, listening.

"Alys," Selendrile's voice called again, fainter, but this time she was waiting for it.

And suddenly Alys knew: Of course he hadn't followed her instructions—he *never* followed her instructions. Instead of staying in the clearing searching for the key, he had started to come after her.

She jumped to her feet and began running down the path, Gower right behind.

She found Selendrile sprawled in the middle of the road, moments away from where she had given up. Without pausing to think, she threw her arms around him and gave him a hug, simultaneously trying to get him to sit up so that Gower could more easily get to the shackle.

He seemed barely conscious and sagged heavily against her. "There's not enough time," he murmured weakly.

"Everything's all right," she said. "Gower's here to help."

That got his eyes open. She felt the muscles in his back and shoulders tighten.

Gower remained out of arm's reach, watching everything suspiciously. His torch cast flickering shadows onto their upturned faces.

There wasn't time to explain it all. Above, the sky was getting pink, and in the forest around them songbirds roused themselves to greet the dawn. "Selendrile," she said, mindful of her promise, "it's all right. Gower and I have come to an agreement. He's a partner now."

"Gower?" He spat out the name.

She gave his shoulder a rough shove. "Enough! I told him I wouldn't let you hurt him."

His expression shifted to something she couldn't recognize, his dragon look. But then he said again, "There isn't enough time."

Gower must have taken that as agreement, for he handed Alys the torch and pulled the file from his belt. "This is *not* as you led me to believe," he grumbled. "He was supposed to be fastened to the stake."

"Just hurry up," Alys said. She lifted Selendrile's right arm and saw that the wrist and hand were bleeding and swollen. Despite her queasiness at the open wounds, she tightened her hug around his shoulders to reassure him. Selendrile shook his head, but she had no idea what he was trying to tell her.

Gower raised his eyebrows when he saw the arm, but wordlessly set file against shackle.

Selendrile flinched at the touch of the metal, sucking in his breath with a hiss.

Of course it had to be iron to cut through iron, but she hadn't thought of it.

Gower looked up, but only said, "Hold the torch steady." He pressed down hard and began moving the file back and forth in a sawing motion.

Alys listened for the snap of metal separating, but there wasn't one. The file put a small dent into the edge of the iron band, nothing more.

Selendrile pulled away from her. "This isn't going to work," he told her, his breathing strained and unsteady. "There isn't time. Don't touch me. You're too close."

"What's going on?" Gower demanded, sitting back on his heels.

"Just cut the shackle." Alys tightened her hold on Selendrile.

After a moment's hesitation, in which Alys watched the sky take on a whole new hue of pink, Gower once again placed the file against the iron band. Alys saw the cords on his neck stand out with the strain, and it seemed his teeth must crack he had them set so tight; but after a massive effort, the file hadn't cut quite halfway through.

Selendrile had his eyes closed as he fought a wave of pain.

Gower flexed his fingers and wiped his hands on his tunic, then once again gripped the file's handle. Grunting with concentration, he cut farther into the iron.

This time Alys thought he was going to make it. But not quite. He stopped just short of severing the band. "Damnation," he muttered, blowing on the palms of his hands.

Before Gower could take up the file again, Selendrile moaned and doubled over.

Alys cast a quick glance at the sky, which showed a hint of blue amidst the pink. She tried to get him to straighten, but he pushed her away. "No time," he gasped.

Gower was suddenly standing up, backing away. He held his hands out, indicating he'd had enough. "That's it," he said. "I'm not getting any closer."

Alys dropped the torch, which wasn't helping anymore anyway, and snatched up the file. There was just a sliver holding the band together. Surely she could manage that. Selendrile was fighting her, and it was only the fact that he was so weak that allowed her to take his hand and saw the file back and forth on the damaged shackle. She closed her eyes against the strain of pressing, pressing, pressing.

Selendrile jerked his arm back at the same instant the band snapped, at the same instant the first ray of the sun fell on her face, at the same instant something slammed into her and threw her, yet again, to the ground.

She opened her eyes to see bits of cloth falling through the air, settling to the ground. *Oh no*, she thought, *oh no*. She closed her eyes quick.

But then she heard something.

An awful cry. Like a huge bird of prey.

Alys jerked her head up in time to see the dragon clear the top of the trees, sunlight glinting on its golden scales. Then with another fierce cry, it disappeared in the direction of the sun.

So much, she thought, for what he thought of her getting a new partner.

Gower made a quick sign of the cross. Then he stood, shading his eyes, staring into the sky. "Yes, well, and thanks to you, too," he shouted into the morning light.

But of course there was no answer.

Chapter 16

ALYS DIDN'T GET Gower back to Saint Toby's by the noonday meal after all, but the fault was his own: He insisted on traveling the rest of the way to the clearing where Alys had originally told him Selendrile would be.

While her common sense warned her he would find the Inquisitor's body where they'd left him, she'd been unable to bring herself to say anything. *Just in case...*, she'd told herself. Just in case, hope against hope, he wasn't really dead and had returned home to Griswold. That was downright stupid. Just in case animals had gotten to the body and carried it off. She couldn't bring herself to think they'd eat it then and there. Just in case Selendrile had had the foresight to remove the evidence. Almost as stupid as hoping Atherton wasn't really dead.

Of course the body was still there.

She hung back, unwilling to approach within clear sight, while Gower crouched beside it. He didn't have to look long to determine what had happened. "Your dragon friend do this?"

Alys nodded. There were explanations, but none seemed adequate.

Gower didn't say any of the things he could have said, either. Instead he told her, "It's indecent to leave his body out like this." So, since they had no tools to dig a proper grave, they gathered stones and piled them atop him, like the old pagan burial cairns that dotted the countryside. It wasn't the Christian rite, but she hoped it was sufficient to set his soul—if he still had one—to rest.

By the time they returned to Saint Toby's— hungry, tired, hands and backs sore, fingernails torn and filthy—the villagers had obviously begun to worry about Gower's disappearance during the night and were setting out to search for him. She saw the look on the face of the first person who recognized her despite the dirt and the boy's clothing, and after that kept her face down. She had thought that it would be easier this time, that—having lived through the past four days—nothing could reach her and nothing could frighten her.

It wasn't easier.

Their hate still tore at her heart.

She was terrified all over again.

Members of the search party, fresh and eager to spread the news, hurried back to Saint Toby's so that when she and Gower reached the center of the village, everyone was there, waiting. Gower, pleased to be the center of attention, had refused to answer any questions along the way. Now, standing with thumbs hooked self-importantly around his belt, he waited for total silence before announcing, "She has something to say."

He had kept his part of the bargain, had proved to be more loyal than Selendrile. But she didn't have to give them any more than the least. "It was true," she said, never looking up, "everything everybody said about me. Then I came back with magic and lies against Gower and his family."

There was a moment of silence, Gower expecting more, the villagers taking in what she'd already said.

"The broken wheels . . . ," Gower prompted.

"My doing."

"My wife and daughter . . ."

"Bewitched. I made an image of myself and put it with Etta's things so you'd blame her for what I did myself."

The crowd was beginning to murmur and stir.

Gower was getting annoyed with this lack of cooperation masking as cooperation. "Tell them about that Inquisitor from Griswold."

"Dead. My doing also. I bewitched the dragon, too, got him to take on human shape to help me hurt you. That's why I came back."

A voice from the crowd said, "That doesn't sound like you, Alys." Risa's mother.

Alys jerked her head up.

Too late.

Four days too late.

Alys pretended the movement had simply been the first part of a shrug. If she didn't let herself believe, they couldn't hurt her. She refused to look up again, answered their questions as briefly as possible, freely took the blame for every ill imagined or real which had befallen the village for the past fifteen years. *There,* she thought at Gower. *There.* She even let him take credit for ridding the village of the dragon. "I killed it," Gower claimed. "It won't be bothering us again," and she let even that pass.

For all that she agreed to everything they said, it took all the afternoon and into the evening for the villagers to decide, as Alys had known they would, that it was up to them to carry out the sentence the murdered Atherton had decreed. The only difference was that this time the method must be more certain.

Another stake was fashioned and set up in full view of the village. Wood was gathered, torches made. *This is what I deserve,* Alys told herself as she let them lead her to the stake, as she put her back to it before they could force her to. Maybe her death would be sufficient repayment for causing Atherton's death in her quest for revenge. But she couldn't bear to watch their faces as they set the kindling about her and called for rope. She set her gaze above their heads, beyond the people to the homes and buildings of the village itself.

And that was when she saw the old witch of the glen, lurking at the edge of the crowd.

It can't be her, Alys told herself. It had to be some other old woman, perhaps Hildy's grandmother, who rarely left the house and got stranger and stranger as the years went by. The old witch had no reason to leave Griswold, having finally acquired a soul to replace her own lost one.

But then the witch saw her looking, and gave a smile of such malicious glee that Alys couldn't fight the truth of it: This *was* the old witch, and the reason she had traveled to Saint Toby's was to watch Alys burn.

It didn't make sense, if it was the witch's soullessness that made her wicked. The only way Alys could work it out was that people couldn't really give up their souls. They only *acted* as though they didn't have one until, eventually, they forgot what it was like *not* to be soulless. Atherton had no more sold his soul to the old witch than the old witch had sold hers to Satan.

Alys watched the old witch come closer and closer, elbowing people aside to stand gloating next to Una in the circle of those closest to the stake. But then Gower came through the crowd also, with the rope to tie Alys, and she had to close her eyes so they couldn't see her panic. She held herself tight to control the shaking.

In her self-imposed darkness, she could smell the pitch as the torches were lit. Gower pulled her hands to the back of the stake. Someone screamed.

Alys tensed even more, assuming that the scream meant an overeager villager had set torch to kindling before Gower had had a chance to bind her.

But then there was another cry of fear.

Before Alys had a chance to open her eyes, she was knocked to the ground, falling into the still-unlit bundles of kindling. The stake, which had broken with a sharp crack, landed on top of her, knocking the breath out of her.

By the time she could see straight, the villagers were fleeing, screaming in terror, Una and the old witch both lost in the panic. Just as Alys got up onto her hands and knees, a blast of wind flattened her again. Her forearms were seized and she was lifted up, up into the air.

But then Selendrile swooped low, so that she could see Gower staggering groggily, too confused to look up. Selendrile dipped so low that

Alys's dangling legs almost dragged on the ground. The rush of air from his wings caused Gower to lose his footing again. He fell, sitting, and Selendrile circled again, close enough that Alys could see in Gower's eyes the moment he realized what was happening, could see him brace himself for the death he was sure was coming.

Which didn't come.

Once again Selendrile took to the air, circling the village, demonstrating to the villagers that there was no hope of outrunning him, no matter which direction they chose. Then again he swooped in close, his wings pulled in tight so that he hurtled between their houses, Alys's feet just barely clearing the street.

He roared, sending flames shooting down the street, licking at the heels of the fleeing villagers. Closer. Closer. Then at the last moment, up and above their heads.

Again he returned to the stake, fallen and abandoned. This time he roared directly at it, and the brittle wood burst into flame whose heat Alys could feel on her legs as they passed over.

Gower had almost reached the edge of the village when Selendrile caught up. He breathed a crescent of flame to block the wheelwright's way, close enough that Gower's eyebrows were probably singed. Gower turned.

Then, with Gower watching, Selendrile breathed fire. Not at Gower, but at the tin shop Gower had fought so hard to possess. For a moment, Alys felt an overwhelming sense of loss for her childhood home.

But only for a moment.

She had seen last night that it was no longer hers. She felt nothing as Selendrile shot over Gower's head and carried her into the darkness of the surrounding night.

AFTER FLYING LONG enough that Alys's arms were beginning to ache, Selendrile let her drop.

She landed flat on her back on ground that was prickly but bouncy. A haystack, she realized, probably the same one he'd dropped her into that first night. She'd given up trying to keep track of how often she'd been knocked down or fallen over in the past day—she probably couldn't count that high anyway.

Selendrile skidded to a stop beside her, transforming to human shape even before the shower of hay settled. He grabbed her by the shoulders, forcing her to sit up, looking intently at her as though searching for something in her face. She saw that his right wrist was almost entirely healed; the left had no mark of the shackle at all. She remembered how he had referred to human bodies as being fragile, and considered, once again, that dragons lived for hundreds of years. It wasn't fair of her to wish he was human just because she was.

"Thank you for rescuing me," she said.

Eventually he let go of her shoulders. Eventually he said, "You're welcome."

The moonlight glinted on his golden hair, long and loose. "So," he said in a voice that gave no clue to his thoughts, "does this mean no more revenge?"

"No more revenge."

He continued to look at her without saying anything.

"I didn't like it," she said. "I felt worse after than before. And I'm very, very sorry Atherton died."

No reaction at all.

"I assume it works out better for you," she

asked, "when you get revenge on those who hurt you?"

His eyes narrowed and his nostrils flared. But he was the one who looked away first. He sighed, shaking his head, probably more at her than in answer to her statement. "Do you want to go back?" he asked.

She thought about it. But then she said, "No. They'll never be able to forgive me."

He looked amused at the thought that she could be concerned with forgiveness. "Then," he said, "is there some other place you'd like me to take you?"

Now Alys sighed. "There were several kind people in Griswold who were willing to take me on. I may go back there." She sighed again. "Or, I could find a new place entirely. I don't think that's as impossible as I used to think it was."

"Ah," he said in that knowing way of his.

Alys rested her head against her knees.

"Or," Selendrile said, not quite looking at her, "you could stay with me."

Startled, she tried to gauge his sincerity from his bland expression. Aware of a hundred reasons why it wouldn't work, she asked, "Do you mean it?"

Selendrile paused to consider. "Perhaps," he said.

"I see," Alys answered.

The dragon-youth took a deep breath. "Yes." He said it quickly and decisively. "Yes, I mean it."

"Well, then," she said, "in that case, I will."